A NOTE TO READERS

While the Fisk and Burton families are fictional, the situations they find themselves in are not. Because Cincinnati was so close to the South, there were many spies who worked in the area during the Civil War.

The families of men who went to fight in the war struggled to survive. Because soldiers had left their regular jobs, their families didn't get money from that source. Soldiers weren't paid much, and often their pay never reached their families. Many women and children went hungry. Cities like Cincinnati hurried to form soup kitchens so that their people wouldn't starve.

The threatened attack on Cincinnati by Southern troops during the summer of 1862 became known as the Siege of Cincinnati. Businesses were closed, and everyone was asked to help build defenses around the city. For weeks during that summer, people lived with the fear that the city they had worked so hard to build was about to be destroyed.

SISTERS IN TIME

Daria
Solves a Mystery
OHIO EXPERIENCES THE CIVIL WAR

NORMA JEAN LUTZ

BARBOUR
PUBLISHING

Cover design by Lookout Design Group, Inc.

Published by Barbour Publishing, Inc., P.O. Box 719, Uhrichsville, Ohio 44683, www.barbourbooks.com

Our mission is to publish and distribute inspirational products offering exceptional value and biblical encouragement to the masses.

 Member of the
Evangelical Christian
Publishers Association

Printed in the United States of America.
5 4 3 2

CONTENTS

CHAPTER 1

Ball Games and War Games

May 1861

Daria Fisk spit into the palms of her hands, which were already sticky with sweat, and worked the warm leather of her baseball.

"Here it comes!" she called to Roy. "Keep your eye on the ball and keep the bat level."

Rearing back for a strong pitch, Daria let the ball fly. It was a little high, which made Roy swing upward to try to connect. He missed by a mile. Behind him, Daria's twin, Andrew, gave a little leap to catch the ball. "I got it," he called out.

Daria heaved a sigh. "Keep it level, Roy," she repeated. "Keep the bat level. Let the ball come to you."

The tall, muscular boy tossed the bat aside in exasperation. "Aw, it's no use. I ain't much good at this."

Daria and Andrew watched as Roy Gartner stomped off their makeshift baseball diamond, walked over to the shade of a big oak, and flopped down on the grass. Though Andrew Fisk was tall for his eleven years, Roy—only a year older—was even taller and more muscular. When Daria and Andrew first met Roy, she thought he'd make a terrific ballplayer. Perhaps she'd been wrong.

Andrew glared at his sister. Picking up the bat, he strode toward Daria. "You can't tell him every move to make," he said under his breath, "or he'll never get the hang of it."

"I wish he could play like the Bradfords," Daria said. "I didn't like their attitudes toward the North, but T. J. and B. J. played a great game of baseball."

The Bradford brothers had been gone for well over a month now. As soon as news reached their family that fighting had begun at Fort Sumter, the Bradfords had packed up and gone back to their former home in South Carolina.

War. The awful word rolled over and over in Daria's mind. She still couldn't believe that the country was calling men to arms to fight against their own people. And a sort of war fever had gripped every person in Cincinnati.

"Well, Roy doesn't play as well as the Bradfords," Andrew reminded his sister, "so we'll just have to make the best of things." He tossed the ball to her, and she reached out and caught it.

Hardly anybody at school wanted to play ball now that the war had started, and it didn't appear this new boy had the ability or the desire to learn.

"All I did was try to tell him to hold the bat level," Daria said, trying to defend herself.

"No one wants to play when they're being bossed around," Andrew said. "You should know that. They especially don't like it when it's a girl doing the bossing."

But Daria had stopped listening to Andrew. She walked over to the grass and sat down beside Roy.

Roy's father, a gunsmith, had moved the family from their home near Columbus. He knew that because of the war, business would be better in Cincinnati, a center for troop movements. The Gartners had arrived in the Walnut Hills area shortly after the war started, moving into a house vacated by yet another family of Rebel sympathizers.

Daria pulled up a blade of grass and chewed on the end. "You'll do better with practice," she said, making a stab at encouraging Roy.

"Maybe," Roy answered.

Andrew flopped down on the grass beside them. "I'm the one who taught him how to play. Maybe I'm just a poor instructor."

Daria picked up her shoes and stockings from where she'd dropped them when the game began. "I'll say."

"Aw, don't be tearing into your brother, Daria," Roy told her. "It's a fairly interesting game. It's just that there are more exciting things to do just now."

"Like what?" Daria stopped pulling on her long stockings and leaned forward, eager to hear news.

The word *exciting* always made her eyes light up. She knew she was a constant worry to Mama, playing baseball and wandering all over town with Andrew. With the exception of getting Daria involved in work for the city's orphans, Mama's attempts to turn Daria into a lady thus far had failed miserably. But Daria didn't care. All her brother's pals liked Daria—and she liked them better than she liked most girls her age.

"Like spying on the troops and pretending like they're Rebs and we're Union," Roy said. "That'd be way more fun than baseball."

Daria knew that all the boys at school wanted to pretend to be soldiers. Even during recess they made pretend guns of sticks, formed into lines, and marched about the playground. Andrew hated the war games, but Daria was grateful to be included in the fun.

"What troops will we spy on?" Daria asked. "It's too far to go to Camp Harrison, and we haven't time to go all the way into town."

Roy jumped to his feet. "I happen to know the Walnut Hills Home Guard is mustering in the park today. That group drills every Saturday afternoon."

Andrew looked at Daria. They knew that, of course. Most of the ragtag group were their neighbors. They hardly considered them to be troops. Andrew stood up as well. "I guess we could go take a look," he said, although he didn't sound excited about the idea.

"Sure we can," Daria echoed. She jumped up and ran ahead.

"Slow down, Daria!" Andrew hollered. "We have to take the baseball gear home first."

"You do that, and Roy and I'll wait here for you."

"Oh, no, you don't. We stick together," Andrew replied.

"But if Mama sees me, she may think of something in the house for me to do."

Daria watched her brother sigh. She read the impatience in his face, and she quickly added, "Go with me partway and wait at the corner. I'll put the things in the carriage house and won't even go in the house. That way Mama won't see me."

Andrew agreed, and they quickly carried out their plan. After stopping by the Fisk home, they hurried toward the park. They could hear the shouts of the recruits from several blocks away. Ever since April, every group of men in Cincinnati that could be called a group had organized into some sort of regiment. Daria marveled that so many volunteers could have been mustered so quickly. Most of the real troops—as Andrew liked to call them—gathered at the fairgrounds seven miles north of the city. The place had been named Camp Harrison.

"I'll be the lieutenant," Roy told them. "Andrew, you be the sergeant, and Daria, you be the corporal."

"Oh, no," Daria protested. "If Andrew's a sergeant, so am I."

Roy pulled off his cap, revealing his unruly straw-colored hair, which never saw a comb. He studied Daria for a moment. Daria knew what Roy was thinking. Most boys never knew what to make of her.

"Tell you what," Andrew said. "I'll be the first sergeant, and she can be the second sergeant."

Roy nodded. "I suppose that'll work. Now we need our guns. Scatter out and look for long, straight sticks."

Once they were armed, they proceeded forward with caution. "If they see us," Roy warned. "We're goners. Stay low."

They crept in a row from tree trunk to tree trunk at the perimeter of the park. At one point Andrew stopped short, and Daria ran smack into his back.

"Oof! Watch it."

"Sorry. I didn't know you were going to stop."

"Shh," Roy warned. "We're getting close." He pointed to a shed with a pitched roof in the backyard of a nearby house. "To that hill, troops," he said. "We'll spy from atop the ridge."

"Yes, sir," Andrew answered.

"Yes, sir," Daria echoed.

As they ran from the trees through the open space to the shed, Daria caught sight of the pitiful group trying to form some semblance of military order on the park green.

One glimpse took all the fun out of the game. The men fell all over one another as they tried to follow the orders of their elected officer, who knew no more about military maneuvers than did the recruits. None had a uniform, though all had on matching red flannel shirts made by the women of Walnut Hills—the twins' mama and older sister Jenny included. Only two of the volunteers carried guns; the rest carried broom handles.

If Daria were a boy and old enough to join, she'd never put in with the likes of these misfits. Instead, she would join the elite Guthrie Grays, like Edward Stephens, Jenny's beau, had done.

Following Roy's lead, Daria and Andrew scrambled up on the roof of the shed. Daria had tucked the hem of her skirt up to allow herself more freedom of movement.

"Stay low," Roy said. "The soldier who sticks his head up might get it blown off."

On their stomachs, they crawled over the splintery shingles of the roof until they could peer over the edge.

"Bang!" Roy said. "I got one."

"Bang!" Andrew said. "My bullet went through two at once."

Daria aimed her stick gun over the edge of the roof. "Bang! I shot the officer, and the whole troop is retreating in mass fear and hysteria."

"That's not playing fair," Roy protested.

"That's my sis for you," Andrew told him. "She has a powerful imagination."

"Hey there!" came a voice from behind them. "You ornery kids get off my shed!"

Daria turned to see a man running across the yard, yelling at them. The stick in the man's hand was larger than any they carried.

"Bad enough I got noisy troops out here. I don't need no mischievous young'uns hanging around here crawling all over my property, causing more disruptions."

In a panic, the three friends scrambled over the point of the roof and down the other side. As Andrew hit the ground, Daria saw him turn to help her, but she ignored his outstretched arms. She sucked in her breath, took a leap, and fell to the ground, her skirts in a wrinkled, mussed heap around her as she rolled on the hard dirt. In a second, she was on her feet.

"Come on, troops. Let's get out of here," she called out to them.

Before Roy knew what was happening, she sprinted right by him. The three raced pell-mell, laughing as they went. Daria put up a good contest, but both boys passed her. It was a dead heat between Roy and Andrew. When they reached the Fisk yard, they collapsed onto the grass, laughing hysterically.

When they finally caught their breath, Roy said, "When school's out next week, let's go out to Camp Harrison and see the real troops."

"That's a long walk," Andrew said.

"We can do it," Daria put in, brushing the grass and dirt from her skirt.

"My papa says there're wagons going out all the time, taking supplies and such," Roy explained. "If we got tired, we could always hitch a ride." Then Roy added, "I heard a boy barely thirteen joined up as a drummer."

"Only thirteen?" Andrew asked.

"I look thirteen," Roy said, still in a serious tone. "I bet I could pass and get mustered in as a drummer."

"You may think you look thirteen," Daria countered, "but you don't really believe you can pass the eagle eyes of the recruiters, do you?"

"A person can do most anything he sets his mind to. That's what my pa always says." Roy's long frame was stretched out on the grass, and he was staring up into the trees. The look in his eyes almost made Daria believe the boy could do what he said.

"You really want to join?" she asked.

"I surely do. I want to show them Rebs a thing or two. They can't just up and fight their own country. They need to be stopped, and I aim to help."

Daria put her chin on her knees and thought about Roy's comments as she surveyed their rambling two-story house with its sweeping apron porch. Through the years, Papa had built onto the house as his family and medical practice had grown. At the end of the front walk was the sign, KEVIN FISK, MEDICAL DOCTOR. The entrance to Papa's doctor's office was at the rear of the house.

"Look there," Daria said, breaking into the solemn moment. "That's Lieutenant Stephens's horse out back."

The two boys craned their necks to see from Daria's vantage point. Sure enough, the lieutenant's fine roan was hitched out by the carriage house.

"What's he doing here at this time of day?" Andrew wondered out loud. Usually Edward Stephens came around in the evenings.

Edward had been courting their older sister Jenny for several months, but ever since Edward joined the Guthrie Grays a few weeks ago, the roan hadn't been hitched at the Fisk home as often.

"We could go ask," Daria answered.

Just then Mama appeared on the front porch. "There you are. Andrew, your papa needs you to hitch Bordeaux to the buggy, and, Daria, I need your help with supper."

Daria groaned.

"Guess I'll be getting on." Roy stood up and sauntered off.

"Will you go to church with us tomorrow?" Daria asked.

When they'd first met Roy, he told them his family didn't go to church much. His papa had always told him church was for women and children. But Daria persisted in inviting him. She informed him that Dr. Fisk not only attended church, but he also prayed with their family every evening.

Sometimes Roy would tag along; sometimes he wouldn't. He gave a little nod. "I reckon I could come. Got nothing else to do. I'll be by early."

Daria nodded at him and waved.

"See you," Andrew called after him. Pulling Daria to her feet, Andrew said, "Come on. At least we'll find out what the lieutenant's doing here this time of day."

CHAPTER 2

War News

Daria saw the look of shock in Mama's clear green eyes as she observed her daughter's disheveled appearance. Mama was every inch a lady with her copper red hair pulled neatly back into a coil of braids at the nape of her neck and her hoop skirts covered with ruffled flounces.

Mama and Jenny sewed dresses for Daria with full-cuff sleeves laden with lace and ruffles and with layers of cloth in the skirts over hoops and petticoats. But when Daria wore them, disaster always resulted. She had heard Mama say to Jenny that she felt fortunate if Daria could make it home from church without mussing her good clothes.

When they came up on the porch, Mama put her hands on Daria's shoulders and turned her slowly around, then shook her head and made tsking sounds. "Daria Ann, how can you get this much dirt on a clean dress in a single day?"

Daria grinned at Andrew and gave a shrug. If Mama had seen Daria on the roof of that shed. . .

"You said Papa needed Bordeaux hitched up?" Andrew asked.

"Mrs. Menken's feeling poorly. Always happens at suppertime," she added, momentarily forgetting about scolding Daria.

Daria started to go in the front door, but Mama said, "Don't go through that way. Edward's with him. Go around outside and knock at the office door like a lady."

"What's Edward doing here now?" Daria asked.

Pushing Daria toward the side door, Mama answered, "That's none of our concern. Now go."

Daria and Andrew did as they were told. As they walked around the house, a fat robin hopped out of their way. Thrushes and mockingbirds were singing in the treetops. Daria squinted up through the thick green branches and stopped to listen to their cheery melodies. Evidently no one had told the birds there was a war going on.

The Fisk home sat on three large lots covered with tall shade trees. A combination carriage house and stable sat to the rear of the lot just across from the apple orchard. Papa's buggy was kept there, and his horse, Bordeaux, was housed in the stable.

As the children approached Papa's office, Edward came out. He shook Papa's hand and smiled. Being part of the Guthrie Grays meant Edward had a full uniform, with brass buttons and epaulets, unlike the ragtag Walnut Hills Home Guard.

Andrew and Daria liked Edward. Even though he was twenty-four and an officer, he never treated them like children. When Edward spied Daria and Andrew, he gave a wave. "Hello, Andrew," he said. "Hello, Daria."

Andrew ran toward him. "Is there an emergency? You're never here this time of day."

Edward shook his head. "No emergency. Sorry I haven't time to chat, Andy, but I've been away from my regiment too long now." The cylindrical dress hat, called a *shako*, with its shiny bill and feathery plume, was beneath his arm. He replaced it now, firming it on and pulling the strap beneath his chin. "Thank you, Dr. Fisk." With long strides, he hurried to his horse, mounted, and rode away.

Daria turned to Papa. "What's he thanking you for? Is he sick?"

Papa pulled off his eyeglasses and gave a wan smile. "I must get my hat and bag and get over to Mrs. Menken's house. Will you please get the buggy ready, Andrew?" He disappeared into his office, leaving Daria wondering.

She trailed after Andrew as her brother headed toward the stable. Bordeaux was a beautiful black gelding with three white stockings and a blaze of white on his nose. Daria got to take care of Bordeaux when Mama didn't need her help, and she looked forward to those times when she had the chance to spend time with the gelding. The one chore she never minded was taking care of the horse. Bordeaux had been a gift from Uncle Jon, Mama's brother, and his wife, Eleanor. Aunt Ellie, as they called her, came from a French family, and she liked to give their horses French names. "Bordeaux," she'd told them, "is a seaport village in France."

Daria wasn't really interested in any village in France, but she agreed that a fine horse like Bordeaux deserved to have a special name. Outside the stable, Andrew gave his special whistle. Soft nickers answered him. Even when Bordeaux was hobbled and grazing in the orchard, he always came when Andrew or Daria whistled. He was a smart horse.

Andrew went into the stall and reached up to stroke the velvety soft nose. "Hello there, fella. Time to hitch up," he said. "Papa needs you."

Sometimes he and Daria saddled Bordeaux and rode him, but they had to stay close to the house in case Papa received an emergency summons. Daria watched as Andrew slipped the halter over the horse's head and led him outside. Opening the double doors of the carriage house, Daria took down the harness from the wall hook inside and handed it to Andrew. As he harnessed Bordeaux, the horse kept trying to reach around and nibble at Daria's arm or shoulders— whatever he could reach.

"You silly thing," Daria said with a chuckle. "Always trying to get more attention."

Papa came out and swung his black bag up into the buggy, then pulled the long reins up to the dashboard. Bordeaux gave a little shake as though he was more than ready to get going.

"Papa, you never said why Edward was thanking you. Is it some sort of secret?"

"Won't be a secret for long, Daria. Edward has asked me for your sister's hand in marriage. I said yes."

Daria stared at Papa for a long moment. *Jenny, getting married?* She didn't know why she felt so surprised, but she did.

"Does Mama know?"

Papa stepped up into the buggy. "I'm sure she's guessed by now. That is, if Jenny hasn't told her." He gathered the reins in his hand to keep Bordeaux from stepping out. "While I'm out, I'll check on the Canfields. The missus is about to have her baby."

Daria nodded, but she was still thinking about a wedding in their family. Jenny had just turned twenty. There were plenty of girls she knew who were younger than Jenny and were already married—some already had babies. The thought of her own self being married in a few years made her stomach feel squiggly. There were too many other things she wanted to do first.

"Muck out Bordeaux's stall," Papa told Andrew. "And after you've had supper, run into town to the newspaper office and see if any war news has come in."

"Yes, sir."

"And, Daria?"

"Yes, sir?"

"You stay home. It's bad enough that you run all over the country with your brother in the daylight hours. These days it's best you stay closer to home after dark." Papa turned to Andrew. "You understand, son? You need to make sure your sister does as she's told."

Daria stuck out her lip, but Andrew nodded. "Yes, sir. I understand."

He avoided Daria's eyes as Bordeaux stepped out smartly, and the buggy rolled out the drive and clattered down the street.

Daria was still fuming at suppertime. It just wasn't fair. She and Andrew were the same exact age—but because Andrew was a boy, he got to have all the fun.

Mirza, their maid, had cooked up a scrumptious ham supper. The thin woman seemed to be all elbows and angles, but she created wonderfully light rolls. Mama scolded Daria for mopping up salty ham gravy with them.

"That's the way a backwoods person would eat," she said. "I've taught you better manners than that." But Daria did it anyway. She was tired of doing as she was told. Besides, there was no better way to get up the last of that good gravy.

While she ate, she studied Jenny's face, but she could see nothing different about her. Jenny spent nearly every afternoon sewing shirts for the volunteers. Surely she knew Edward had come by, but her face was a smooth mask. Jenny favored Mama not only in manner but also in her fair skin and copper-colored hair. Papa often made Mama blush by saying the two looked more like sisters than mother and daughter.

Now Jenny and Mama chatted away about who had brought their sewing machines and who was helping with the work. But Jenny, who was soon to become a bride, looked the same as she always had.

As Daria polished off a second helping of Mirza's apple cobbler, she pushed back her chair and sat poised while Andrew told Mama that he was supposed to run to town to check on the war news.

Mama looked worried, but she only nodded. "Be careful." Then she turned back to her conversation with Jenny. Daria stood up and began to clear the dishes from the table. She waited until Mama had her hands in the sudsy dishwater, and then she asked, "Do you mind if I go out to the stable? I want to spend some time with Bordeaux."

Mama nodded absently. Clearly, her mind was on other things, and Daria seized her opportunity. She slipped out the back door and ran as fast as she could toward town.

After a few minutes, she had caught up with Andrew. He must have heard her footsteps behind him, because he turned around, frowning. "Papa said I was to go alone, Daria."

"I don't care." Daria stuck out her chin. "It doesn't make any sense that you're allowed to go and I'm not."

Andrew opened his mouth to argue, but then he just sighed. "You're going to get us both in trouble," he muttered. But Daria knew that Andrew was glad to have her there. They had gone everywhere together ever since they were born, and it felt strange to both of them now that their parents were starting to insist that Daria had to stay home when Andrew went out.

Daria decided to divert Andrew's mind to other thoughts. "Want to see if Roy can come with us?" she asked.

Andrew nodded, and they turned down Woodburn Street. Here, the houses were closer together. Andrew hurried up the steps of the two-story white house and knocked on the door. Mrs. Gartner answered the door, balancing a baby on her hip. She smiled when she saw Andrew with Daria behind him. Compared to their mama and older sister, Mrs. Gartner dressed rather plain, but she was always friendly to Daria and Andrew.

"Howdy, Andy," she said kindly. "Howdy, Daria. You come for a visit?"

"Papa's asked me to go downtown to check on the war news," Andrew said. "May Roy come with us?"

Roy appeared at the door, looking over his mama's shoulder. His face brightened at the invitation. "Can I, Ma? Can I?"

Roy had told Daria and Andrew that Mrs. Gartner was a bit frightened of the big city of Cincinnati. "Why, even Columbus was too big for Mama," Roy had said. "She grew up in the woods, not the city."

Now, Mrs. Gartner hesitated a moment, shifting the baby on her hip. Then she said, "Oh, I don't see no reason why not." She turned to her son. "You go on. But mind you, don't get all angered up just 'cause the news ain't too good."

"I'll try not to," Roy answered and ran to fetch his cap.

As they walked down the hill toward town, Roy apologized for his behavior that afternoon. "Seems I ain't much as a ballplayer," he said. "It appears you put a lot of store by the game. I didn't aim to be a disappointment to you."

Daria was sorry then that she'd been so impatient with their friend. "It's a sore spot inside me," she explained. "Our teams at school were getting pretty good. Not to sound puffed up, but my pitching was improving a great deal the past few months." She kicked at a rock in the street. "Then the stupid war had to come and ruin everything." But she knew it wasn't just the war. It was the way Mama and Papa were suddenly insisting that she couldn't do the same things Andrew did.

"Don't worry, Daria. Once I become a drummer and help the Union soldiers march into battle, we'll make quick work of this 'stupid war.' "

"You ought not talk like that, Roy," Andrew said. "About joining, I mean. You'll worry your mama worse than she's already worried."

"You don't think I say anything in her hearing? I just keep my mouth shut and bide my time."

"What about your papa?"

"Papa works long hours at the gunsmith's. Says there's enough work to last for months. We hardly seen him since we came to the city. He sure enough won't miss me."

Daria didn't know Roy well enough to judge if he was just talking—or if he was talking truth.

When they arrived at the *Gazette* office down on Third Street, the lights were glowing. Since the war had started, it seemed no one in the city slept. Something was always happening. The news that would be printed in the next day's early edition was usually posted in the window. As they approached, Daria saw the headline: COLONEL ELMER ELLSWORTH SLAIN!

"Colonel Ellsworth," Andrew muttered.

"Someone you knew?" Roy asked.

Daria turned to Roy. "You've not heard of Ellsworth?"

Roy shook his head.

"He came through Cincinnati last year when Abe Lincoln was campaigning here. He was Lincoln's bodyguard. Our uncle Jonathan met him."

Roy's eyes grew big. He turned again to study the headlines, shaking his head.

"He was commander of the Zouave Cadets," Andrew said. "His was the first outfit to invade the South."

Daria thought about the handsome young man with the long, wavy, dark hair. He'd been no older than Edward. And now he was dead. Shot by a Rebel. How Daria hated this horrid, horrid war.

CHAPTER 3

The Wedding

As Daria, Andrew, and Roy walked slowly back to Walnut Hills, Andrew explained how Uncle Jon had been a law partner with Salmon Chase before Mr. Chase became secretary of the treasury in Lincoln's cabinet. Because of this, Uncle Jon and Aunt Ellie had attended a tea given for Mr. Lincoln when he was running for president.

"My uncle knows a lot of important people," Daria said.

"Wow," Roy said, duly impressed. "Were you there? Did you meet Old Abe?"

"Mama tells us we should call him Mr. Lincoln. And no, we weren't there."

"Mr. Lincoln? That does ring more respectful. I'll call him that, too."

"And even if we didn't meet Mr. Lincoln," Andrew said, "we saw him and heard him speak. He's a good man."

"Wow," Roy said again. "None of the boys back home know anybody who's seen the president."

Late that evening, the Fisk family gathered in the parlor for prayers. No one had missed Daria, and now she was trying not to feel guilty about disobeying Papa. *But it wasn't right,* she told herself. Surely God must understand that Mama and Papa weren't being fair.

The parlor's heavy velvet draperies were pulled back, and the windows had been left open to let in the cool spring air. The big piano sat in a corner of the room, with Mama's secretary standing by the windows. A cluster of chairs, a couple of settees, and the davenport were clustered nearer the fireplace. Papa sat in his upholstered chair with the Bible in his lap, his eyeglasses in his hand.

Andrew and Daria settled into separate corners of the davenport. The quiet and peace of the moment enveloped Daria like a quilted comforter on a winter evening. The thought of a gallant young man named Elmer Ellsworth dying for his country seemed so remote here in the safety of the family parlor.

When Papa asked for the news, Andrew told what he'd read in the window of the *Gazette*. "The Union forces had taken the city of Alexandria, Virginia," Andrew explained. "Lieutenant Ellsworth went upstairs in the inn where the Confederate flag was flying to pull it down. When he came back downstairs, carrying the flag, the owner of the inn shot him."

Mama winced and shook her head. "So young," she said softly.

"I remember him," Daria said quietly. "It's hard to think of him being killed."

"Edward has told me about Ellsworth," Jenny put in. "How he'd gone about the country rallying men for his elite militia while everyone else was saying there'd never be a war."

"In his youth, he had more foresight than many of us older folk," Papa said. "But enough about the serious news. We have a note of good cheer much closer to home."

Daria glanced at Jenny and saw her blush. Papa explained about Edward's visit that afternoon and that he'd asked to marry Jenny. "Knowing the fine, upstanding young man he is, how could I say no?" Papa smiled warmly as he looked about his family.

Andrew went over and hugged his sister. "Jenny, I'm so happy for you."

Mama also went to Jenny and put her arms about her daughter.

"He's a fine young man, Jenny. I feel sure the Lord brought the two of you together."

Daria was quiet. She wanted to scream out, "But what about the war?" None of them seemed to want to admit that Edward would be leaving with his regiment any day. What kind of marriage would that be?

Papa looked at her and said, "Daria, don't you want to wish your sister well?"

Daria walked over and put her hand on Jenny's shoulder. "Best wishes, Jenny. I'm real happy for you and Edward." She hesitated. "Does Christian know?"

"Now how could Christian know when I just learned it this afternoon?" Papa asked.

"He'll find out soon enough," Jenny said.

Christian, their eighteen-year-old brother, worked for the Little Miami Railroad. They didn't see much of him because the trains were constantly on the go, transporting troops and supplies.

Papa called his little family back to order and read the Scriptures and prayed, asking God to bring a quick end to the awful conflict.

That night as Daria slept, she dreamed of a young officer coming down a flight of steep stairs with a Confederate flag wadded in his arms. A shot rang out; the man fell. But in her dream, the face of the officer belonged to Edward. When Daria awakened, her heart was beating fast and she was shivering. She hated the thought that something so bad could happen to Edward and to her sister Jenny.

Roy had no nice church clothes. Mama insisted it didn't matter. And Daria agreed. But some people still looked askance at him. As the pastor explained how Jesus died for everyone, Daria could see that Roy was listening with rapt attention. She wondered if Roy understood about how to ask Jesus into his heart, but she didn't want to embarrass her and Andrew's new friend by asking.

Daria didn't have to. On the way home from church, Andrew explained to Roy God's plan for salvation. Roy looked interested in what Andrew had to say, but Andrew didn't push things, and Daria was glad. She was proud her twin had the courage to speak up for his beliefs—but she didn't think it seemed right to try to shove them down Roy's throat. She tried to think of something more she could add to what Andrew had said, but it seemed to her like he had said everything that was important. Besides, she wasn't too sure how she felt about God these days. She could never decide if He was on her side—or Mama's and Papa's.

The following Monday morning, Daria sat staring out the school window, longing to be anywhere but in the classroom.

Her fifth-grade teacher, Miss Epstein, had been teaching at the Walnut Hills Grammar School for almost as long as the school had been open. She had a sharp eye and seemed to know whenever Daria's mind began to drift, which was quite often. Daria felt stifled and bored in school. Fortunately, she received high marks in all subjects without having to study much. Andrew wasn't so lucky. His mind often wandered like Daria's, but it seemed as though no matter how hard he studied, school was a struggle for him.

Miss Epstein rapped on her desk with the long map pointer. "I have an announcement to make," she told the class. "I'm afraid the news is not good."

Behind her hung the map of the United States. Miss Epstein had put colored pieces of paper on the states that had seceded from the Union since April.

"Due to the attention being given to war matters, there will be no commencement day celebration as in other years." This news brought loud groans from the entire class. "The school superintendent," she continued, "has decided that only graduations will take place."

Daria glanced across the aisle at Andrew. She could see he was as disappointed as she was. School commencement exercises were a highlight for every student, with parades, recitations, music, and a big picnic. Now, just like that, it had been canceled. It was as though those mean Confederates were coming right into their classroom and ruining everything.

At recess, as usual, the fifth- and sixth-grade boys played soldiers. They voted for officers and then drilled and marched as though it were the real thing. On several occasions they had invited Andrew in. "You'd make a great officer," Daria had heard one boy tell him. But Andrew ignored their pleas and continued to carry his ball and glove to school each day. Daria faithfully played catch with him, but she wished the boys would ask her to play. As much as the war scared her, it also made her feel excited. It was just one more thing confusing her. Everything was changing. She worried that before too long, everything she enjoyed most was going to be ruined.

As they were tossing the ball back and forth, Roy surprised them by asking to join in. "I like playing soldier a lot," he said, "but I'd like to learn more about this game of baseball."

Andrew smiled and removed his leather glove. "I'll even let you wear the glove."

They made a three-cornered catch game, and by the time recess was over, Roy was beginning to get the feel of both the ball and the glove. Daria smiled. Maybe everything wasn't totally ruined, after all.

Papa was happy with Daria's marks at the end of school. He wasn't so happy about the grades that Andrew received. Daria knew Andrew felt terrible that he'd disappointed Papa.

"At least you know I didn't cheat," Andrew said lamely.

"I'm certain you'd never cheat," Papa said, "but I'm also certain you're not putting forth the effort that's needed."

Daria wished she could explain to Papa that Andrew did try to listen and pay attention. But nothing at school interested him. Nothing except baseball. She knew that the only thing Andrew wanted to do when he grew up was form a team in Cincinnati like the teams he'd read about back East—the Knickerbockers and the New York Nine. How much book learning would a person need for organizing a baseball team?

"I want you to promise me that when you begin sixth grade, you'll make a greater effort at excelling in your studies. A man can do little these days without a good education."

Andrew and Daria both knew how many years Papa had studied to become a good doctor. Daria saw Andrew looking at the medical books that lined the walls of Papa's office. "I'll try harder next year," he said. "I promise."

"Very well, then." Papa put his eyeglasses back on. "You may go now, both of you. I believe Bordeaux needs you, Andrew. See if your mother needs you, Daria."

Daria scowled, but this time she did what her father said.

Jenny and Edward's wedding took place in the family parlor on a Saturday afternoon in the middle of June. Daria had a new dress, but the starched ruffles made her itch. The worst part was that she'd have to get up the very next morning and put on a fancy dress again for church.

Mama and Jenny had spent long hours finishing Jenny's dress on time. Even Daria was asked to help put on the last few touches. Then there were food preparations for the formal sit-down dinner that evening.

Edward had been granted a short leave, and Uncle Jon offered to let the couple stay at his cabin just outside of town until Edward had to report back again. Then Jenny would come back home. Daria knew that if there were no war, the two would be fixing up their own home.

While Daria was helping with last-minute details with the dresses, Andrew had been put to work that morning moving furniture in the parlor so that everyone could be seated. Fresh-cut flowers were everywhere, and their sweet aromas floated on the air. Shuble, their new gardener, seemed to have a magic touch in the flower garden.

By one o'clock, the knocker began sounding at the front entrance. Soon the house was full of happy, chattering folk—friends, neighbors, and relatives. Aunt Eleanor and Uncle Jon were there along with Daria's three younger cousins. Christian had gotten the day off from the Little Miami Railroad. Three officers from Edward's regiment were in attendance, looking spiffy in their uniforms.

A dear friend of Mama's, Mary Ellen McClellan, whose husband was leader over all the Ohio volunteers, was there. Mama's younger cousin, Martha Burton, had taken leave of her hospital work with the Sisters of Charity and had agreed to stand up with Jenny.

Mama had sewn Daria's dress as well. Made of forest green silk, it swept the floor just like Mama's and Jenny's did. Daria had heard Mama and Jenny saying it was time Daria began wearing long dresses. "After all," Jenny had reminded Mama, "she is almost twelve." Daria liked the way the green made the red highlights in her hair shine and glow. But she hated how stiff and proper. . .how downright ladylike the dress made her feel.

Papa quieted the crowd and asked everyone to be seated. Pastor Parcells stood by the piano while Mama played a nice hymn. Edward stood by the pastor and waited. Presently, Jenny came down the open stairway. The crowd murmured their approval at her cream-colored dress covered in lace. Daria had to admit she'd never seen Jenny look more beautiful. She walked forward with Martha at her side. They stopped beside Edward.

Daria shifted slightly from side to side. She tried to stand so that her ruffles didn't scratch so much, but she felt nervous as a cat. How she wished she were out in the stable with Bordeaux. But the ceremony was over almost before it began. Daria glanced away as Edward Stephens held Jenny and kissed her in front of everyone, after which Pastor Parcells announced to the crowd, "I present to you Mr. and Mrs. Edward Stephens." Everyone cheered.

The wedding was over, but Mama said Daria still couldn't change out of her new dress. What's more, she was ordered not to spill anything on the green silk.

The parlor furniture had been moved out of the way and the rug rolled up, allowing the guests to dance through the afternoon until supper was served at the long table in the dining room. Daria didn't dance. She sat stiffly at the edge of the room, scratching her legs where her petticoats rubbed against them.

Everything was changing all at once. Jenny getting married. . .the war. . .and her new, grown-up lady's dress. It was just too much for a body to stand all at once.

CHAPTER 4

Edward Leaves

The day Edward was scheduled to leave Camp Dennison—June 24—
the skies were gray and dreary and the weather cold and damp. The
camp was situated seventeen miles from Cincinnati on a level of
ground midway between the gentle rise of hills on the north and the
Ohio River on the south. Nearby, the Little Miami River snaked
down through the hills to meet the Ohio. Hugging the shoreline was
the Little Miami Railroad line.

The camp had been laid out by McClellan and Rosecrans before
either became generals. Edward had explained to Daria and Andrew
that the location was strategically perfect, with plenty of water and
access to the rail line.

Looking at the rows of dismal wooden barracks and the sea of
mud that was supposed to be a parade ground, Daria wondered how
it could be a perfect anything.

Since the wedding, Edward had been able to see Jenny only a few
times. Then, night before last, word came to Jenny by messenger that
Edward's regiment was scheduled to board the train and leave for
Virginia early on the twenty-fourth.

The Fisk home had been filled with gloom ever since the news
arrived. Even Daria and Andrew were quieter than usual. Though
Jenny tried to be strong, her eyes were red much of the time. She was
quiet and somber.

Papa assured her no matter who needed his services that morning, he would make sure she was at the camp when the troop train departed. He was true to his word.

Papa drove the buggy as near to the camp and the tracks as he could. Others from town had ventured out in the rain to see the boys off, but it was a small group. Troop movements in the busy port city of Cincinnati had become an everyday occurrence in the three months since the war began.

Andrew and Papa wore their rubber rain slickers and stood outside the buggy watching as the uniformed troops lined up in the rain to board the train. Mama, Jenny, and Daria stayed beneath the protective covering of the buggy.

"Don't they look smart in their new blue uniforms?" Mama asked.

"They do look fine," Papa replied. "Edward was worried that the uniforms wouldn't arrive before they had to leave."

"Did he mind giving up his uniform of the Guthrie Grays?" Daria asked Jenny.

"The new ones are much more practical for the field." Daria heard Jenny's voice break just a bit on the words.

Christian had been assigned to work on the train. In May, word came that all railroad workers were exempt from serving in the army, since the railroad was so vital to the war effort. At first, the family was relieved that Christian wouldn't have to fight. Then they'd learned about Rebels sabotaging the tracks to wreck and derail any and all Union trains.

Daria was convinced no place was safe anymore. A few days earlier a rumor had spread through the city that Rebels planned to blow up the Cincinnati waterworks and set fire to the city. People panicked. The rumors proved untrue, but fortification plans in the city were sped up considerably.

Daria's thoughts were interrupted by the sight of a figure standing up on the tender car, waving wildly.

"It's Christian!" Andrew whooped. He stepped away from the buggy, threw back his slicker, and waved both arms. Papa waved, too, and Mama waved her handkerchief. Everything inside of Daria wanted to bolt down that hill toward the railroad and demand that Christian come back to them. To stay home and stay safe.

Papa reached beneath his slicker and pulled out a pair of field glasses. Handing them to Jenny in the buggy, he said, "Perhaps you can pick out Edward in the crowd with these."

"Oh, Papa," she breathed. "Thank you." She stood up in the buggy to scan the long lines of soldiers. Daria stood as well and held her parasol over her sister's head. "There he is!" Jenny exclaimed. "I see him! The third car. Look at the line beside the third passenger car."

Daria looked and there, clearly, she could tell it was Edward. The young officer was looking their way and waving. All of them began to wave and shout. Others in the crowd by that time were doing likewise. As a fresh torrent of rain cut loose, the last men were loaded and the whistle sounded. With clouds of black smoke belching from the smokestack and steam hissing, the wheels of the train began to turn, and it lurched forward. Little by little, the train picked up momentum, its shrill whistle echoing off the hills behind them.

The family waited in the rain until the last car disappeared around a curve far down the track. Daria heard Jenny sniff, and she knew her sister was trying to choke back tears. Papa reached inside the carriage and patted Jenny gently on the shoulder. "Come on, son," he said over his shoulder to Andrew. "Let's get these ladies out of this terrible weather."

By July, Cincinnati had given more than five thousand of its young men to the war. The streets reflected it. Each time Daria and Andrew went into town to learn the war news, it seemed another shop had closed because a man had gone off to war. Other businesses folded due to the blockade against shipping to the Rebel states. Companies that formerly sold thousands of dollars worth of goods in the South suddenly had no customers. Many of Papa's patients were unable to pay their bills.

And then there were the families left behind by the soldiers. The city council set up a fund to assist those women and children who now had no income.

In spite of the prevailing sadness, the city pulled out all the stops for a gala celebration of Independence Day. Daria was thankful for it. She and Andrew were up and dressed before dawn. Mama had given them permission to go to Mount Auburn for the early fireworks display. Of course, they stopped by Roy's house first.

Roy, too, was up early, excited about the full day of events just ahead. When he answered the door, he said, "Wait just a minute. I have something to show you."

He ran back inside and came out carrying a small wooden crate with a rope attached to it.

"What is it?" Daria asked.

From behind his back he presented two carved sticks. Putting the rope over his head and propping the crate against his stomach, he said, "A drum! This here's my drum."

"Well, I'll be." Andrew reached out a hand to touch the contraption.

Daria thought it looked to be great fun. "Let's hear you play."

"I've been doing a powerful lot of practicing," Roy told them as he moved down the steps and off the porch. "Watch this." He began to march about the yard, tapping out a steady rhythm.

Andrew and Daria clapped their hands. "You're every bit as good as any drummer I've ever heard," Daria exclaimed.

He then showed how he could play reveille, taps, and the call to attack. "I know how to play retreat, but I don't care to play it as much."

Daria thought Roy was clever to create his own drum.

"May I try?" Andrew asked.

"Sure." Roy pulled the rope over his head and handed it over, then showed Andrew the proper way to hold the drumsticks. Try as he might, Andrew just couldn't quite get the hang of the rhythm.

Daria wanted to try, but just then she glanced up at the sky and saw that dawn was breaking. "We'd better hurry, or we're going to miss all the fun," she told them.

"Are we taking this with us?" Andrew asked as he handed back the drum.

Roy shook his head and put the drum and sticks on the porch. "Not now. But when we come back from watching the fireworks on the hill, I want to take it with us to the parade."

"A fine idea," Andrew agreed. "Come on. Last one to Mount Auburn Street's a rotten egg!"

The fireworks against the early morning sky made a breathtaking sight. But hearing them burst and seeing the blazing lights as they exploded made Daria think of Edward going off to fight where real shells were bursting, real guns were firing, and real men were dying.

Later, all the military companies of the city turned out in full regalia for the parade through the downtown streets. There were the Independent National Guards, the Mount Auburn Rifles, the Gymnasium Light Guards, the Pearl Street Rifles, and the Teachers' Rifle Company. At the head of the column marched the Cincinnati police force in full uniform. Andrew, Daria, and Roy ran beside the parade through the crowds lining the streets. Roy's drum echoed the rhythms of the marching bands.

The parade ended at the public landing. Bands played, speeches were given, and a large Union flag was hoisted up the brand-new, hundred-foot flagpole. When the cannons were set off, cannons from Newport Barracks and from the town of Covington across the river echoed a retort. Sounds reverberated up and down the river valley.

As Daria listened, she studied two steamboats at the boat works that were being converted into gunboats. Five-inch oak bulwarks walled them in, transforming the lovely open vessels into floating forts. Everywhere Daria looked, she saw reminders of the war.

When Major Robert Anderson stepped up to the podium to speak, the crowd went wild. The major had been the commander at Fort Sumter before it fell to Rebel hands. He told of the days of holding out against the Rebel forces and how their small group of Unionists had fought hard, though isolated in the fort.

As cheers went up from the crowd, Daria marveled at the courage and daring of this leader and his men. The major described the howitzers, mortars, and cannons brought in to destroy the fort. More than three thousand projectiles had been shot at them in less than two days.

The major's brother, Larz, lived at Third and Pike Streets in Cincinnati, and the major had come to the city to rest before being sent once again into battle. He was given a hero's welcome. As he closed his speech, the handsome, clear-eyed major offered up a prayer for the war to end quickly.

When the speeches were over, the crowd moved outside of town to Taylor's Grove for a picnic. In years past, the festivities had been held at the fairgrounds north of town. But that area was now Camp Harrison, where rows of tents housed the recruits. The entire grandstand had been enclosed to create officers' quarters. Taylor's Grove was the next best place for a town celebration.

Later in the day, as people rested beneath the shade trees from their ample picnic lunches, bands played lively music. Footraces were set up according to age. Andrew proudly won three different heats in his age division, beating out Roy in two of them.

Roy was impressed by Andrew's speed. "I'd like to see you make a home run and fly around the bases in a real baseball game," he said.

The comment suddenly made Daria wistful in spite of all the fun. "You'll see my brother do just that, Roy Gartner. You just stay around after this old war's over, and you'll sure enough see it!"

Chapter 5
Bull Run

The news each day was filled with problems in and around the landing. Officials appointed by the city to guard the docks were on the lookout for illegal goods. It was against the law to send food, arms, or horses to the South, and the city jail was full of persons who tried to do so. Rumors of smugglers and spies spread through the city like wildfire. The entire city was on edge.

A few days after the Fourth of July, Papa again sent Andrew into town for the news, but since it was daylight, he didn't seem to mind this time if Daria went along, too. They learned that the steamer *Westmoreland* had just docked. The ship was full of bullet holes. For a moment Daria was frozen, staring at the dispatch posted in the window.

It seemed impossible that an ordinary passenger steamboat would be fired upon. Since the landing was only a few blocks from the *Gazette* office, Daria and Andrew decided to go see for themselves.

Prior to the war, as many as twenty boats would be docked at one time; but on this day, the landing was almost empty. Daria and Andrew made their way through the crowd of curious onlookers already gathered there. As they pushed to the front, they saw the captain pointing out the holes—large holes—to anyone who would listen.

"They weren't just shooting with rifles, either," he exclaimed. "See them holes? They had some mighty big guns lobbing shells at us." He shook his head sadly. "Seems as though the days of quiet river runs to New Orleans is about over."

"He done better than the *Neptune* and the *Ohio Belle*," a man beside Daria remarked. "At least he come home with his boat. Them others warn't so lucky."

The man was right. The two boats he named had been taken over by Rebel soldiers. Passengers had been forced to get off and find their way home the best way they could.

Daria stared at the holes in the beautiful steamer. Anger rose up inside her. How dare they? How dare those Rebels shoot at innocent people? It made her want to go get a gun and fight those crazy Rebs. Clenching her fists, she followed Andrew home. She knew her twin was as angry and upset as she was.

When the twins reached their house, a buggy Daria didn't recognize was parked in front of the house. "We'd better go in the side door to the kitchen just in case it's dressed-up company," Andrew said.

In the kitchen, they found Jenny helping Mirza arrange refreshments on a tray.

"Who's here?" Andrew asked. He helped himself to a small sandwich off the tray in Mirza's hand.

Jenny slapped his hand. "Take one from over there." She pointed to the counter. "These are all arranged just so. And besides, your hands are dirty."

"Who's here?" he asked again, taking a sandwich—a bigger one—from the counter. Daria grabbed a sandwich, too. She thought Jenny looked white and tense. But then, she nearly always looked that way lately.

"Mrs. McClellan and Cousin Martha," Jenny answered.

"A social call?" Daria took a big bite of the sandwich. It seemed that ever since General McClellan had received his appointment to be commander general over the entire Union army, Mary Ellen McClellan had spent quite a bit of time at the Fisk home.

"Sort of. Mary Ellen—Mama says I may call her by her given

name—seems to need someone to talk to. Some people in town aren't even speaking to her because they don't like the way her husband's handling the war."

"How silly." Andrew finished off his sandwich in two bites.

"Also, Martha and Mary Ellen are forming their own soldiers' aid society." Jenny turned to Daria. "You're invited to take part, too."

Daria nearly choked on her last bite of sandwich. "Me? In a soldiers' aid society?"

"Oh, Daria," Jenny said, her voice going all soft. "I never knew what all a soldier needed just to fight a war. They need warm mittens and flannel drawers for winter, and mosquito netting and socks and all sorts of things. But the hospital—the hospital has even more needs, and the government isn't allowing any money for the military hospital. Can you imagine that? They need sheets and pillow sacks and bandages. All sorts of things."

Just then Mama peeked through the kitchen door. "Jenny, what's keeping you? Oh, hello, Andrew and Daria. Did you ambush the sandwiches?"

"Coming, Mama," Jenny answered. Turning back to Daria, she said, "We need you."

Daria felt funny inside. She wished she hadn't gulped down the sandwich quite so fast. She turned and met her twin's eyes, but for once she couldn't see what Andrew was thinking. Did the soldiers really need her?

Early in the evening of July 22, church bells and fire bells sounded. News flew through the city of a mammoth battle fought at a place called Bull Run the day before. The first dispatches led everyone to believe that the Union, led by General Irwin McDowell, had made a swift victory.

But the celebration was premature. When the real facts followed, people discovered just the opposite had happened. The Confederates had soundly defeated the Union forces, sending them into a frantic retreat. The newspapers from back East called it the "Great Skedaddle!"

"How could that have happened?" Roy asked in disbelief as he, Andrew, and Daria stood in the crowd outside the *Gazette* office.

Andrew shrugged. "Beats me. I thought everyone said we'd polish 'em off at the first swipe." Andrew craned to see the latest dispatches in the window.

"Almost five hundred dead," Roy said through his teeth. "Those Johnny Rebs'll be sorry for this. We'll show 'em. Next time we'll whup 'em all the way down to the Gulf."

"I wonder if the list of casualties is in yet." Daria couldn't keep her mind off Edward. Christian had been back in the city for a week or two and had had supper with the family one evening. But he could never stay long. The work of transporting troops and supplies was never ending. At least they knew that he was away from Bull Run. But the last Jenny had heard from Edward, he had written that he was leaving Washington, D.C., to join McDowell's men.

Just then a clerk came to the door of the *Gazette*. "Names of casualties haven't come through yet," he told the crowd. "Possibly in tomorrow morning's edition."

Daria looked at Roy and Andrew. "We might as well go home. We need to tell Papa the latest."

The devastating news was almost more than Daria could stand. She'd been sure after one fight that the Rebs would be put in their place for good. It hadn't turned out that way at all.

Daria, Andrew, and Roy hardly spoke as they walked slowly back toward Walnut Hills. When they came to the street where they parted ways, Roy paused at the corner. "Somebody needs to teach them Rebs a lesson."

Daria nodded. "You're right. I thought sure our forces would do it. See you tomorrow, Roy."

"See you." Roy turned and walked away.

At the house, Daria and Andrew went right to Papa's office with the news. Fortunately, there were no patients there. Papa took off his eyeglasses and pressed his fingers against his eyes. "What's it all coming to?" he said softly. Slowly, he stood up and put his arm over his youngest children's shoulders. "Let's go tell your mama and sister."

When Jenny heard the news, she went flying to her room in tears.

The rest of the evening was quiet. Daria went to the stable to comb and brush Bordeaux. Andrew joined her and oiled Papa's harnesses. Bordeaux's company seemed to soothe them both somehow. Andrew pulled a tack box over near the stall and sat on it as he worked oil into the harnesses to keep them soft and supple. Bordeaux stuck his head over the stall door and nickered and nodded, enjoying the children's company. No one said a word, yet Daria could feel worry hanging in the air between them. Bordeaux nuzzled each of the children, as though he understood every word that was not said.

Early the next morning, Daria went downstairs for breakfast before either Jenny or Andrew.

"Good morning, Daria," Papa said. "I'm pleased to see you're up so early." He was in the dining room drinking his coffee. Daria smelled frying ham and heard Mirza in the kitchen helping Mama with breakfast.

"Good morning, Papa." Daria's stomach grumbled with hunger.

"Andrew has to help me fix some things in the office today," Papa told her. "So I want you to go to town and bring home as many different newspapers as you can find. Perhaps with several, we can find at least one with a complete list of the dead and wounded from Bull

Run. The sooner we know, the sooner Jenny can regain her peace of mind."

Daria nodded, feeling warm and proud that for once Papa was sending her instead of Andrew. "Want me to go now?"

"If you would, please." Papa smiled. "I'm sure Mirza can give you a ham-and-biscuit sandwich to take along."

"Yes, sir."

Daria hurried into the kitchen. After greeting her mama with a kiss on her cheek, she said, "I'm going into town early. Papa asked me to."

Mama nodded, her face solemn.

"Guess you want a bite to take along?" Mirza asked, taking a light, fluffy biscuit off the tray at the sideboard. Steam rolled out of it as she cut it in half and piled on several slices of frizzled ham. Handing Daria the fat sandwich, she said, "Bless you, child."

"Thank you, Mirza." She stuffed a bite in her mouth and ran out the door.

She was sure Roy would be up, so she hurried to the Gartners' house first. Roy would be good company on the walk. She'd just finished off the last bite of the sandwich when she got there. Wiping her hands on her handkerchief, she walked up the porch steps and rapped on the door.

Mrs. Gartner opened the door, still dressed in her wrapper. Her eyes were red, and she was wiping her cheeks with a handkerchief. "Oh, Daria, there you are!"

"What's the matter, Mrs. Gartner? Is someone sick? Or hurt? Does someone need Papa?"

"It's Roy, Daria." She pulled a scrap of paper from her pocket. "He ran off in the night to join the army. He's gone, Daria. My boy is gone!" She broke down in heavy sobs.

CHAPTER 6

Papa's Decision

Daria studied the note Mrs. Gartner had handed to her. It wasn't true. It couldn't be true.

"He's. . . ," Daria started. "He's too young. They'll send him back."

Mrs. Gartner pressed the hankie to her mouth and shook her head. "They're taking drummers at most any age. I know. I read about it. And Roy taught himself all the military calls. He can play them all tolerably well."

That was true. Roy had practiced constantly on his crate drum. He was very good. The forces needed good drummers.

Daria thought back to past conversations. "He said yesterday that somebody needed to teach the Rebels a lesson because of Bull Run."

Mrs. Gartner nodded. "He said the same words to us. But we never dreamed he'd up and leave. Mr. Gartner's almost beside himself with grief."

Daria suddenly remembered that Papa and the rest of the family were expecting her back home with extra newspapers. "Excuse me, Mrs. Gartner, but I must be on my way. Jenny's husband was at Bull Run, and we still have no word on whether. . ." She couldn't finish the sentence.

"I understand. You go on. Please, let me know if you hear from Roy or know of anyone who's seen him."

"I promise I will. In fact, Andrew can ride to Camp Harrison and ask around for you."

Mrs. Gartner managed a smile through her tears. She reached out to touch her shoulder. "I'm obliged to you, Daria. Much obliged. I'll keep your family in my prayers."

"And we will pray for your family, as well."

Daria's head was reeling as she turned to walk back down the steps. How could Roy have done this to her? Leave without even confiding in her, without saying good-bye? And she'd thought they were friends. Daria just hoped that this didn't give Andrew any ideas to do the same.

Downtown, the newsboys were standing on the corners, waiting for their bundles of papers. Daria went to the *Gazette* office to see the newest dispatches. There were more devastating details about the retreat from Bull Run. She scanned the list of dead and wounded. The name Stephens wasn't among them, but it wasn't a complete list.

As Papa instructed, Daria bought about half a dozen newspapers. With her hands full, she returned home.

When she walked into the dining room, Jenny was there. She took one look at Daria's distraught expression and said in a quivery voice, "Did you find Edward's name?"

"What is it, Daria?" Papa asked gently. "You look upset."

Daria unloaded the newspapers in front of Papa. "It's Roy."

Andrew came into the room just then. "Roy? Is he sick?"

"He ran away to join up."

Andrew seemed to waver where he stood, as though Daria's news had hit him like a blow. Mama came over and put her arms about him. "I'm so sorry, Andrew. I know you two were becoming close friends."

Andrew nodded. Daria could see the tears in his eyes.

"Maybe he's out at Camp Harrison," Papa suggested. "He'd be easy to locate."

Daria nodded. "I told Mrs. Gartner that Andrew could go look for him there."

"Good idea," Papa answered.

"But breakfast first." Mama led the family to the table where she and Mirza had set breakfast.

After looking through all the papers, Papa finally found as complete a list as could have come in so soon after the battle. No Stephens was listed, but several soldiers were still reported missing.

Jenny was somewhat comforted, but she was still worried about Edward's safety. "I won't breathe easy until after a letter comes," she said.

Daria and Andrew ate halfheartedly. Their appetites had fled. Before going out to feed Bordeaux, Andrew turned to Daria. "Are you coming with me to help find Roy?"

Usually Daria was jumping up to go before he even asked. This time, Daria glanced at Jenny. "I'd like to," she said, "but they're expecting me at the sewing circle."

Andrew nodded, jumped up from the table, and hurried out to the stable. A few minutes later, as he was brushing and grooming Bordeaux, Daria came into the stable.

"I want to go with you," she said softly. "Mama and Papa said I could. It's just that. . ."

Her voice trailed away. Andrew kept brushing Bordeaux's coat, his eyes staring straight ahead. "Maybe you're starting to like the idea of turning into a lady." His voice sounded as though Daria had betrayed him.

"No! It's not that." Daria searched for the words to express what she was feeling. "When I'm running stitches in one of those shirts or knitting woolen socks," she continued slowly, "I can almost see a soldier wearing what I've made. Or when I'm hemming a pillow sack, I can almost see a soldier in the military hospital putting his tired head down on the sack that I made."

Andrew kept brushing, though he'd already done a thorough job. Daria wanted to add that it was sort of nice being with all the women. Some of them talked to her as though she were another grown-up

46

lady, like she was one of them. But she couldn't say that to Andrew. He would think it was a sign that she was giving in to their parents' efforts to separate them by turning Daria into a lady.

"Come on," she said. "Let's get going. We have to find Roy."

Andrew climbed up onto Bordeaux's back, and Daria scrambled up behind him.

Camp Harrison, unlike Camp Dennison, was made up mostly of tents. It had not been created for permanent use. Situated due north of the city, it was close to the Cincinnati, Hamilton, and Dayton Railroad line. Andrew and Daria followed the tree line near the tracks to stay out of the glaring July sun. They stopped periodically to rest a moment and drink from the canteen they'd brought along.

When they reached the camp, they were stopped by a sentry. "Let me do the talking," Andrew whispered to Daria.

"We're looking for our friend, Roy Gartner," he explained to the sentry. "He ran away last night to join up, but he's just turned thirteen."

The sentry leaned on his gun. "Lots of 'em doing that." He shook his head. "I got a young'un myself at home. Sure wouldn't want him running off. Your friend want to be a drummer?"

Andrew nodded. "He's learned all the commands, and he's good. Could you help us locate him?"

"Wait here till my replacement comes," he said, "and I'll take you to headquarters."

The replacement arrived within the hour, and the sentry did as he promised. In the renovated grandstand were makeshift offices with men bent over desks littered with stacks of papers. Andrew inquired again about a new recruit, a young boy who would have arrived within the past twenty-four hours—but there were no new recruits of the age Andrew described.

"Perhaps he went out to Camp Dennison," the young man at the desk said. "They're leaving out of that camp more quickly than they are here."

Andrew and Daria had planned to go there next. Andrew nodded his agreement.

"Or," said a soldier at the next desk, "the fastest way for him to slip away and be mustered in is to catch a ferry to Covington and join up there."

Kentucky. Of course. Daria hadn't thought of that. The state of Kentucky just across the river still hadn't decided whether to go Union or Confederate.

"Thank you," Andrew told the men, and he and Daria turned to leave. They were escorted to the perimeter by the same soldier who'd brought them in. "Sure hope you find your pal," he told the children as they climbed up onto Bordeaux's back.

The next day, Daria and Andrew went down near the landing to the Little Miami Railroad Station, looking for Christian. Fortunately, their brother was loading large crates and barrels from the platform onto a boxcar. Daria explained about Roy leaving and her promise to Roy's mother to help find him. Christian gave a nod.

"This here's a quick run out to the camp and back to deliver supplies," he told Daria and Andrew, motioning toward the train. "I'll talk to the engineer about letting you ride along."

It was a favor Daria hadn't expected. If their mission weren't so serious, riding in the engine with Christian, Andrew, and the engineer and fireman would have been a thrill. But now all she could think of was Roy.

The word they received at the headquarters of Camp Dennison was the same as at Camp Harrison—no young boy had recently tried to join up as a drummer. Dejected, Daria went and got water for the railroad workers while Andrew lent a hand to help Christian and the other workers unload the heavy cases of supplies before the train made its return trip to town. It looked more certain than ever that Roy had gone to Kentucky on the ferry.

Daria dreaded breaking the news to Mrs. Gartner. She had hoped they would find Roy and that he would change his mind and come back home. However, telling Roy's mama wasn't as bad as she'd thought. Mrs. Gartner had come to terms with the fact that Roy wasn't coming back anytime soon.

"I've prayed for hours," she told Daria and Andrew. The baby was on her hip, and a toddler tugged at her skirts as she talked. "At last, in the wee hours of the morning, I was able to let go and turn him over to God's hands." She gave a weak smile. "Which is what the Almighty has required of me anyhow. And now I have peace. Bless you both for trying."

As Daria and Andrew walked home, Daria thought about Mrs. Gartner's words. "Andrew, it must be a very difficult thing to do."

"What is?" Andrew asked quietly.

"Saying good-bye to someone you love so much. To let go of someone you care about. I wonder if Jenny could ever do that with Edward." Daria doubted that Jenny could. And she wondered if she and Andrew could let go of Roy as Mrs. Gartner had. Daria wasn't sure she was much good at trusting God. It was hard enough convincing herself that God would work out the war and her growing up—she found it even harder to believe that He would take care of Edward and Roy.

As July bled over into a hot, dry August, Kentucky continued to waver on the issues. There were rumors that if Kentucky went with the Confederate states, Rebel troops that were massing at Camp Boone in Tennessee would quickly march northward and take Cincinnati.

Daria read Kentucky governor Beriah Magoffin's statement in the newspaper: "We will furnish no troops for the wicked purpose of subduing our sister Southern states."

Kentucky's refusal to send any troops to either cause infuriated most people in Cincinnati, Daria included. She couldn't understand why it was taking the people of Kentucky so long to make up their minds.

A tidbit of good news arrived in late August. Two forts at Hatteras Inlet in North Carolina had been taken and secured by the Union navy. The good news, though, came after more bad news: Union commander Nathaniel Lyon had been killed in a small battle at Wilson's Creek in Missouri. Other than that, not much was happening—anywhere. After the humiliation at Bull Run, General McClellan decided his troops needed more training.

The end of August brought letters from both Roy and Edward. With a letter in her hands in Edward's own handwriting, Jenny seemed to change overnight. She was her old self once again.

Daria, however, did not feel better after reading Roy's letter. In it, Roy apologized for having left without telling Daria and Andrew. He had taken the ferry to Covington and joined up. Then he was shipped to Virginia to catch up with the Ohio regiment.

The other soljers treat me with respect. We don't do much 'cept march and drill. And then we drill and march some more. But the soljers are training with old muskets, which they call "Old Brown Bess." They was made afore you and me was ever borned, in 1828. Ain't no wonder they run from the Rebs. They shore do need new rifles. Word is we'll get some afore the next battle.

The soljers say I'm a fine drummer. Bout the best they ever heard play. Hope you ain't sore at me for running off like I did. But I aim to show them Rebs a thing or two, God willing. I sure could use a letter. Mail is hankered after almost more than food. But then the food ain't nothing special. Not like my mama's cooking is.

I've wrote to Mama and Papa to let them know where I was. I tole Papa he was wrong about God being for wimmen and children. Men gettin redy for battle pray a lot.

Yore fren, Roy

Daria and Andrew were in the stable as Daria read the letter out loud. Daria had pulled it out from the other mail picked up in town, and Mama and Papa didn't even know that it had come. Folding the letter back into the envelope, she sat on the tack box for a time not moving, trying not to think what might happen to Roy when he went into the heat of battle. She sure hoped God knew what He was doing.

Daria was excited that September was just around the corner. School would start soon, and she loved school. But their birthdays were also coming up on the nineteenth. Daria almost wished she could skip the year and move on to age thirteen—or else stay eleven forever. The age of twelve was nothing. She felt stuck between girlhood and woman-hood, like a wagon stuck axle-deep in a mire of mud, unable to move either forward or backward.

Their sixth-grade teacher was Mrs. Voorhees, whose husband had gone off to war. Many of the men teachers were gone, and that meant several married women had come in to take their places. Mrs. Voorhees seemed kind enough, but right away the rowdy students learned they could take advantage of her. Daria loved being back in the classroom, but she hated all the noise and disruption there. And she knew Andrew felt like a caged animal.

About a week into the new school year, Daria and Andrew arrived home from school one afternoon to find three horses hitched near the carriage house. One was unmistakably Uncle Jon's favorite mount. The other two were fitted with military saddle and gear.

The children admired Uncle Jon's horse and then went toward the house. As they were crossing the yard, the door to Papa's office opened, and the men came out.

Daria recognized one of the officers as General Rosecrans, or "Rosey," as he was affectionately called by his men. The other officer was a stranger. Uncle Jon waved a hello.

"Afternoon, Daria, Andrew. Wish we could stay and visit, but we're in a hurry to catch a train."

Daria nodded and stared as the men mounted and rode off. What would a general be doing at their house?

Papa was standing in the doorway of his office. Daria felt her mouth go cotton-dry as she went to her father's side. She didn't like the strange look in Papa's eyes.

"What is it?" Andrew asked. "What did they want?"

Something deep in Daria's gut told her what was coming before Papa ever spoke the chilling words.

"They need doctors desperately, childen. The general came to offer me an officer's rank and to ask that I join the Union forces." Papa stopped a moment and put his hand on Daria's shoulder. "I said yes."

CHAPTER 7

Papa Goes to War

Everything inside Daria wanted to scream out in protest. Not her papa. Let everyone in the whole world go to the war, but not her papa. How would they live without Papa's strong presence there to hold them together?

"Come on, children," Papa said softly. "Let's go tell your mama."

Papa asked Mama to join them in the parlor, and then he closed the doors. Jenny was still in town at the sewing circle. Daria moved closer to her mother as Papa repeated his terrible news. Mama pulled her close beside her on the davenport. As much as Daria wanted to cry, she knew she had to be strong like her mama. Now was not the time for tears.

Mama looked up at Papa. "I know you must go," she said. "I've known you would go. It was just a matter of time."

Daria could hear the strain in her voice, but she was amazed that Mama sounded as calm as she did.

"They've offered me rank as a captain," Papa told them. "Imagine me, an ordinary doctor, becoming a captain."

Summoning a slight smile, Daria said, "You'll be the smartest-looking officer in the whole Union army."

Papa smiled. "Thank you, Daria. I appreciate those words."

Daria couldn't help but wonder what they would do. Even officers—who made more wages than enlisted men—had very small salaries. How would they live without Papa's income? She tried to shut out visions of standing in line at the soup kitchens with other needy families.

"When will you be leaving?" Mama asked.

"A week from today."

Daria heard Mama's breath catch. "So soon?"

"Before our birthdays," Daria added weakly. She glanced at Andrew.

Papa nodded solemnly. "General Rosecrans told me that since Kentucky has finally joined the Union, troops will be building up in that area. I'll be needed there."

Kentucky. Somehow that didn't sound so far away to Daria. Not as far away as Virginia, or Washington, D.C., or Bull Run, where so many soldiers had died.

"I was going to head over to the sewing circle," Daria said. "Should I tell Jenny? Or should I wait and let you and Mama tell her?"

"You may tell her," Papa said. "You may go now if you wish, Daria. I know the ladies are waiting for you to join them."

Daria rose to go, then ran to Papa's chair, leaned down, and hugged him as tightly as she could. He gently stroked his youngest daughter's hair.

The night before Papa was to take the ferry to Newport Barracks, he gathered his family about him so they could pray and talk together. Papa had hoped Christian would be in the city, but he was back East with another trainload of troops and supplies. They seldom knew Christian's whereabouts anymore. Would it be that way with Papa, as well?

Papa instructed Daria to take good care of Bordeaux. "You can ride him," he said. "In fact, I want you to keep him fit. Let Andrew take care of the tack and help with combing and brushing. Bordeaux is important to him, too. Be sure to help your mama, too. She'll depend on you."

Mama nodded, smiling, and Daria also nodded, not trusting her voice.

"Andrew, I expect you to stand by your mama and help her as much as possible. You'll be the man of the family now."

Mama looked at Andrew and smiled again.

"Work hard to bring your grades up," Papa went on. "You may be tempted to slough off just because I'm not here, but don't yield to that temptation."

Daria knew Andrew was struggling with his classes more this year than ever before. "Yes, sir." His voice was barely a whisper.

"What about your patients?" Jenny asked.

"The older doctors will have to take over the load," Papa told her. "Most of them are as capable as the younger ones."

Daria didn't believe that for a moment. Papa's patients loved him dearly and trusted him completely.

As Papa spoke words of love and encouragement to each of them, Daria could almost feel Papa's love pouring over her like ointment.

Picking up the family Bible, Papa turned to the Twenty-third Psalm and read it aloud. When he came to the verse, "Though I walk through the valley of the shadow of death, I will fear no evil," Mama began to weep softly, for the first time since Papa's news.

Finishing the psalm, Papa looked up from his reading and removed his eyeglasses. "This world is fleeting and temporary," he told them. "Our real home is in heaven. Never forget that. I may be called to help preserve the Union, but my higher call is from God." He looked at each of them. "That is your call, as well. We cannot afford to allow hate to rule our hearts."

When he said the last part, he looked right at Daria and Andrew. *Does Papa know how much we hate those Rebels who started this crazy war and disrupted our entire life?* Daria wondered.

Papa prayed then, asking for God to watch over him and guide him and also for God to protect his family in his absence. Then he prayed that none of them would allow hate to rule their hearts.

When he looked up again, his eyes were filled with tears. "We'll have no need for a lot of words at the landing in the morning. The important things will have been said here tonight."

"I love you, Papa," Daria said as she again ran to Papa's side. Jenny joined her.

After a moment, Papa stood, looked at Andrew, and opened his arms. Andrew stepped across the room and clung to Papa. Daria wished they never had to let him go.

The next morning, sodden gray clouds hung over the city. Jenny commented that God was weeping with them in their sorrow. Daria agreed. She'd never felt such searing pain as she felt now.

Papa did look smart in his uniform. But no amount of uniform would make Daria's papa look like a fighting man. Papa was too gentle to fight. He would be there to relieve suffering—that which he was best at doing.

They'd been able to get word to Christian, and he joined them at the last minute, having come from the Little Miami station. Papa embraced his elder son, just as he had his other children the night before.

Captain Kevin Fisk managed to give a brave smile to his family as he stepped aboard the ferry steamer. They stood in silence as the whistle blew and the gangplank was pulled up. Foam bubbled up around the paddle wheel as the steamer slowly moved out across the great Ohio River to the Kentucky side.

Daria and Andrew took turns looking through the field glasses until the ferry landed near the large compound of brick buildings known as the Newport Barracks, which had stood there since territorial days. Papa would be there only an hour or two before catching a train south, deep into Kentucky.

Papa must have sensed they were still watching, for when he stepped off on the other side, he turned and waved one more time. Officers met him at the landing and escorted him up the hill toward the headquarters building.

Then the Fisk family said good-bye to Christian, as well, since he had to hurry back to the station. Andrew helped his mother and sisters into the buggy and turned Bordeaux toward home.

Later, after Andrew had removed the harnesses from Bordeaux and Daria was brushing the animal's sleek side, the two children put their arms about the horse's neck, rested their heads against the horse's warmth, and let their tears flow unchecked. Bordeaux barely twitched a muscle. Somehow, Daria was sure the horse understood exactly what they were feeling. Bordeaux's patient love comforted her, and for just a moment, she felt as though God was there with them in the stable. *Dear God,* she prayed silently, *please bring Papa home safe. And Edward and Roy, too.*

Mama and Mirza put together a nice evening dinner for Daria's and Andrew's birthday. They didn't really want a party, but Mama insisted that they celebrate their birthday as though nothing had changed. Daria couldn't help but feel that it seemed all wrong to celebrate without Papa there.

Mama invited Mary Ellen McClellan and Lucy Hayes, wives of Union generals. Of course, the Burtons were part of the celebration. Mama felt the younger cousins—Donald, Elaine, and Jon Jr.—could liven things up and that the generals' wives needed the company. She was right on both counts.

The twins received several nice gifts, which they both appreciated, but then Uncle Jon said he had a special surprise for Daria and Andrew.

"For us?" asked Daria.

Dark-haired Elaine, who was barely seven, was bouncing all over the place. "We have a surprise for you, Cousin Daria and Cousin Andrew," she said. "But you have to come outside." She was tugging at Daria's hand.

Daria looked at Mama, but Mama just smiled. Did she know?

When everyone had gathered outside, Uncle Jon lifted a beautifully tooled saddle and bridle from his carriage.

"Your papa purchased this from me before he left," Uncle Jon said. "He wanted me to present it to the two of you on your birthday."

Daria could scarcely believe it. They had an old saddle that had been around as long as she could remember. It was nothing close to the quality of the tack that Uncle Jon owned.

"Just like Papa," Daria heard Andrew say, his voice breaking.

Daria ran her hand over the smooth leather. He was right. It was just like Papa. Knowing that Papa had planned this for them before he left made the ache of missing him even more painful.

As autumn turned cooler, days began to drag. Daria was feeling worried. Andrew spent more and more time alone. He spent most of his spare time riding Bordeaux. He often rode clear out of town to get away to where it was quiet and peaceful. Daria was hurt that her twin didn't seem to want to be with her the way they always had before. It was just one more awful change in her life.

She worried even more when Andrew stopped asking her to join him on trips into town to get the latest news. Rather than walk to the *Gazette*, now he rode into town to get the news. But there was no news.

The war had turned into a non-war. No one was doing anything.

Daria tried to keep busy with school, her sewing circle, and the soldiers' aid society. Mary Ellen McClellan often came to the house in tears, weeping over the wicked things that were written about her husband in the newspapers. Some were calling General McClellan a traitor because he wouldn't order his troops to fight.

At school, Daria did well, but Andrew's marks fell. Daria knew that all he wanted to do was be with Bordeaux and sit in the saddle that Papa had given them. Andrew couldn't seem to shake the weight of sadness that both twins continually felt. Daria knew he felt guilty about his promise to Papa to work hard on his studies, when he just couldn't seem to concentrate on his schoolwork.

"Andrew, I can help you with your homework if you want," Daria offered one afternoon while they were taking care of Bordeaux.

Andrew just shook his head.

One October afternoon when Daria and Andrew arrived home from school, Mama came to meet them. Her face was grim.

"Is it Papa?" Daria asked, her heart in her throat.

Mama shook her head as she led the way down the hall. "I want to talk to you about your low marks in school, Andrew."

Andrew's shoulders slumped. "Oh, that." Daria thought he sounded relieved.

"You make it sound as though grades and studies are not important," Mama said. Daria knew she didn't understand how scared both twins had felt when they saw their mother's tight face.

How could Daria make their mama understand? Andrew was doing the best he could. She looked sideways at her brother, but he was staring down at his dirty fingernails, and she knew he could think of nothing to say in his own defense.

"What is it, Andrew?" their mother persisted. "Why are your marks falling lower?"

Andrew shrugged.

"Nothing at school really matters," Daria said, trying to explain her twin's feelings. "I mean, what use is it to learn about literature and elocution and mathematics when the entire country is at war?" She looked at Mama, wishing she had the power to erase the disappointment from her face. If only she could understand that both twins felt as though school was a waste of time these days.

Then Andrew lifted his head and spoke in a choked voice. "Do you realize that most all the older boys have either gone off to fight or are working at the foundry?"

"And what does the war have to do with you and your grades?"

"Soon I'll be the only boy in school above fifth grade."

"And if you are, what of it? When you are where God wants you to be, that's all that matters."

"How do I know if that's where God wants me?" he asked.

Daria wondered how Mama could be so sure about what God wanted. Maybe God would want Andrew to be helping the war effort. The very thought made her feel cold all over.

"First of all," Mama said, "God wants you to obey your parents. Your papa and I feel strongly that you must get your education, be there a war or not."

Of course, Andrew and Daria both knew that. But somehow, as they got older, Daria was finding it harder and harder to be as obedient as she once had.

"I'll try harder to pay attention in class," Andrew said grudgingly.

"I can help him," Daria offered.

Mama's face relaxed just a little. "Thank you, Daria. Will you work with your sister, Andrew?"

"Yes, Mama," Andrew muttered, but Daria knew his words were

a halfhearted promise. Her brother just couldn't grasp things the way she did. Her heart ached for her twin, but she didn't know what else she could do to help him.

"I trust that you will keep your word," Mama said. "It's what your papa would want."

Thanksgiving was spent at the Burtons' fine home, located a little farther up in Walnut Hills. Uncle Jon was too old to fight in the war, and Daria was almost jealous that her cousins still had their father at home. She couldn't help but think that if Uncle Jon hadn't been on a first-name basis with General Rosecrans, perhaps Papa would never have been called up. And though she knew it was wrong and wasn't what Papa would want, bitterness was growing inside Daria.

By the time December rolled around, money was scarce for the Fisk family, and Daria made a decision. She would quit school and begin working as a seamstress. The women in her sewing circle were always telling her how fine her sewing was. Even in a time of war, there was always sewing work to be found. Daria knew that money was tight for the family. If Daria took a job, she could help Mama and the family with the finances. Mama was always telling her she had to grow up. Well, if she had to grow up, Daria decided, then she should take on some of the responsibility for helping out the family.

Mama had already dismissed Shuble, the gardener. With the strained family budget, there was nothing extra to pay the man's salary. Daria knew it broke Mama's heart to let him go just when the gardens and yards were looking so fine. They all knew that Mirza might have to go, as well. But if Daria had a job, then perhaps they could keep her.

The family continued to gather in the parlor every evening for prayers and Scripture reading, though often Daria's heart was not in it. In the evenings, more than any other time of day, she missed Papa the most. She'd rather go on up to bed than sit with the family and bear the ache that wrenched at her insides.

The week before Christmas, Daria's plan was complete. She'd talked to Mrs. Wellington, a local dressmaker, who was interested in taking Daria on as a seamstress's helper. It would be a start. Daria was sure that she would be a full-fledged seamstress in no time. Daria decided to tell Mama what she was going to do that night during prayers.

Before Mama opened the Bible that evening, she said to her children, "I have something I want to discuss with you." Her voice was clear and steady. "As you know, our budget is strained almost to the breaking point. Even our savings is being quickly depleted. I have no way of knowing at what point your papa will be able to send money to us. But it's my belief that God gives us ways and means by which we can remedy adverse circumstances."

Daria felt almost smug. After all, she had the solution to the family's problem. Mama was leading right to the subject of which she wanted to speak. Then her mama shocked her clear down to her toes.

"We have a great number of rooms in this rambling old house. And so," Mama said, smiling at each of them, "I've decided to turn our home into a boardinghouse."

CHAPTER 8

The Fisk Boardinghouse

No one spoke. The silence was deafening. Daria looked at Andrew. His eyes were wide with disbelief.

"I know it may take a little getting used to," Mama said into the silence, "but I've thought about it. I believe this is the best solution to our financial situation."

Jenny cleared her throat. Jenny, who usually sided with Mama, was now hesitating. "A boardinghouse? That seems like rather drastic measures."

"My dear Jenny, we live in a time that calls for drastic measures."

"But, Mama," Daria protested, "strangers in our house? What would Papa say?"

"Why, Daria Ann," Mama said, "our home has always been open to guests—only now they'll be paying to stay. I've been making a few notes that I'd like to share with you."

She rose, stepped over to her secretary, and pulled out sheets of paper filled with notes and figures and lists. It was obvious she'd been doing a good deal of planning.

"I'll need help from each of you in order to care for our guests properly," Mama continued as she came back. Carefully arranging her hoops, she sat down in Papa's chair next to the roaring fire. "With this plan I hope to be able to keep Mirza working for us."

"What about my work with the sewing circle and the soldiers' aid society?" Daria asked.

"You may have to rearrange your schedule somewhat," Mama said gently. "But I'm sure after your chores are done here, you'll still be able to help the war cause by knitting and sewing with the others."

Daria didn't look entirely convinced.

"Now," Mama said, smoothing out the sheets of paper on her lap, "Jenny, we'll move you in with Daria. That will free up your bedroom."

Andrew looked upset. "Mama, you're not planning to rent out Papa's office, are you?" Daria knew that Andrew often went into the office to sit still and soak up Papa's presence. He didn't want anyone touching anything in that office.

"No, of course not, Andrew. What I planned was for you to turn the waiting area into your own room. We can put a cot in there for you, and we'll use your room as another rental room."

Andrew released a silent sigh of relief. Daria felt a little jealous. Sleeping in Papa's office might be kind of fun for a change—but she would have to share a room with Jenny.

"This will be our first step. Your two rooms along with the guest room will give us space for three boarders. If we find we're able to handle yet another guest, I'll move downstairs to the smaller parlor and rent out the master bedroom. From my figures, I believe renting three rooms will provide sufficient income for the time being. Now, let's see. . ." Mama shuffled the papers for a moment until she found what she was looking for. "Ah, yes. Here's the list of chores each of us will have to do to make our guests comfortable and to keep our home in good order."

"Can't Mirza do all that?" Andrew wanted to know.

Daria was wondering the same thing.

"Oh, my, no," Mama said. "Stop and think—Mirza will now be cooking for three more people. Meals will have to be served on a schedule."

Daria couldn't imagine such a change. Because Papa was often called away from the house to treat a patient, lunch and dinner had often been served at odd hours. Sometimes they would wait on Papa; other times they wouldn't—there was never a set time for any meal. This habit had continued after he left for the war.

Mama handed each of them a separate sheet listing which days they were expected to do which chores. Jenny didn't say a word. Andrew let out a loud groan. Daria felt like melting into the floor. According to her list, she was supposed to help serve supper, sweep out rooms, make the beds, shake rugs, and empty chamber pots. How was she supposed to go to sewing circle? She had come up with a plan to help with the family's money problems, and now she was supposed to be a maid! What a crazy turn of events!

"When do you plan to open your new business?" Jenny asked, studying the list Mama had handed her.

"I thought just after New Year's Day would be nice," Mama replied. "I plan to place an advertisement in the classified section of the *Gazette*. We can also put a sign out front."

Nice? Daria wondered how Mama could use such a word to describe this terrible situation.

"Now, if there are no more questions," Mama said, setting the papers aside and opening the Bible, "I believe we should pray."

Early the next morning, Daria went to Jenny's room and knocked softly. At Jenny's bidding, she opened the door and slipped inside, hoping Mama wouldn't be coming down the upstairs hallway.

Jenny was still in her wrapper. "Good morning, Daria," she said. "To what do I owe this visit at the crack of dawn?"

"I have a question to ask."

Jenny sat down on the edge of her featherbed and patted a place beside her. "Come and sit down." When Daria was settled beside her, Jenny said, "Ask away."

"What do you think of Mama's boardinghouse scheme?"

Jenny studied Daria a moment, making Daria feel uncomfortable. "What do you think of her 'scheme,' as you call it?"

"I don't much like the idea of having strangers in our house. And I sure don't think much of having to do all this extra work." She didn't bother to hide her disgust at the thought.

"Tell me, Daria, what would you have us do while Papa is away?"

Daria took a deep breath. "I was. . ." She hadn't planned to tell anyone her own idea, but Jenny had asked. "I sorta thought about quitting school and going to work."

If her statement surprised Jenny, Daria couldn't tell. Her older sister touched her arm. "That's a noble and caring plan, Daria. It shows me your heart is in the right place. I know Mama would say the same thing. But what would Papa say? Had you thought of writing him and asking his opinion?"

That thought had never occurred to Daria because she knew Papa would never want such a thing.

"I know your answer from your silence," Jenny continued. "Do you think Mama's happy about this decision? This is more difficult for her than for any of us, Daria. Never forget that."

"But she seemed so pleased with the idea," Daria protested.

"She's making the best of a very unpleasant situation, just as we all have to do." Jenny paused a moment. "Daria, I have always dreamed of becoming a wife and having my own little place where I could cook for my husband and greet him at the close of each day. I never dreamed I would get married and then be alone in my parents' home." She sighed. "There's nothing any of us can do about the circumstances we are in. But we can find ways to bring cheer to one another in spite of the circumstances. If we really try, we can see a little bit of good in most everything."

Jenny put her arm around Daria's shoulder. Daria could smell the fragrance of her lilac water. "Mama is being strong and courageous. Can we do any less?"

Daria could only shake her head.

"It will take courage and determination for you to do the work Mama has asked you to do. Keep in mind as you're shaking the rugs and sweeping floors that you are making Mama's load a little lighter. And that's what Papa would want of you."

Unable to speak, Daria stood and quickly left the room. Jenny was right. But how Daria hated this terrible war!

Christmas had always been Daria's favorite time of year. She couldn't remember ever having a sad Christmas. Not even the year she and Andrew had the measles. Had it always been Papa who made everything so full of life and fun? Because with Papa away, the life seemed to have gone out of everything.

Mama decided that they would not purchase or make Christmas gifts for one another. Instead, they would present gifts to the benevolence storeroom at church. Gifts given to that cause went to the needy families of the hundreds of volunteer recruits who had gone off to war.

"There are so many people in the city worse off than we are," Mama pointed out. "It's important that we think of others at this special time."

On Christmas Eve, they gathered in the parlor and wrote special messages of love and encouragement to Papa and Edward. As the cold winter winds whipped around the house, Daria's thoughts also went to Roy. She was certain that Andrew was thinking about Roy, too. There had been no more letters from their friend since the first one they had received. Was Roy sleeping out on the cold ground on Christmas Eve? Daria felt a pang of guilt for wallowing in self-pity. At least she had a warm home, a wonderful family, and good food to eat.

As at Thanksgiving, they spent Christmas Day at the Burton home. Aunt Ellie had invited a vast number of guests, and their spacious home was filled with music, laughter, and scores of people. One could almost forget there was a war at all. In spite of the good food and company, though, Daria was relieved when the day was over.

Early the next morning, Mama set all of them to work moving furniture and scrubbing every corner of the house. She had borrowed a cot from the Burtons, and they placed it in the reception room of Papa's office. Andrew then brought most of his belongings downstairs from his room and turned the place into his new bedroom. From the reception room window, he could look out and see the stable door directly behind the house. Daria knew he was already imagining being able to sneak out in the night to spend time with Bordeaux.

Even with Mirza's help, it took the better part of the day to complete the work involved in getting their home ready for boarders. That evening Mirza made a delicious oyster stew from tinned oysters they had on hand. It was a special treat because items that used to come up the river from New Orleans, such as coffee, sugar, and seafood, were in short supply. Everyone was so weary from the day's work that there was little conversation as they ate.

"Tomorrow," Mama said, "we'll sort through the linens to be sure we have enough for each room. Some pieces may need to be laundered and ironed. Andrew and Daria, you may take my advertisement to the *Gazette* in the morning."

"Yes, ma'am." Since there was so little news these days, Andrew had stopped going to town every day. But Daria knew he was always glad for an excuse to saddle Bordeaux and go somewhere, and Daria would be relieved to escape the house for a little while, as well.

That night Daria lingered in Andrew's new room, reluctant to settle down upstairs with Jenny. Andrew had his own little heating stove, which made the area quite cozy. There was a bowl of apples set on a small table by the door. Andrew grabbed an apple from the bowl and grinned at Daria. She knew what he was thinking, and together they slipped out in the cold to the stable.

Andrew gave a low whistle, and Daria heard Bordeaux answer. "Hello, Bordeaux," she said as they stepped into the darkened stable. She moved to the stall and reached up to pet the velvet nose. Bordeaux snuffled softly, nosing around Daria's hand. "He wants his treat," she said over her shoulder to Andrew.

"Did you think we forgot, Bordeaux?" He brought out the apple and offered it on his palm. "Mama says we're spoiling you. But I don't care."

Bordeaux made noisy crunching sounds as he devoured the apple. Juice dripped from his mouth.

"I'm your next-door neighbor now," Andrew said to his horse. "All you have to do is look out your window there, and you'll be able to see me. And I can open my window and call good night to you."

He reached up to rub Bordeaux's ears and run his fingers through the silky mane. "When it gets warmer, I can leave the window open, and we can talk to one another across the way. Would you like that?"

Bordeaux nodded just as though he understood every word, and Daria giggled. She was convinced the horse did understand.

"Nice as that would be, I'm believing Papa will be home long before it gets warm again. Long before." Andrew heaved a big sigh that seemed to come from the very depths of his soul.

The twins stood together silently, shoulder to shoulder by the big horse. After a long moment, Daria sighed. "Good night, boy. We'll be out to saddle you early in the morning. Mama wants us to take the advertisement to the *Gazette*. She doesn't ask us to get the news anymore. There's no news to get."

With that, Daria and Andrew slipped back across the yard to Andrew's new sleeping quarters. Daria watched while Andrew crawled into the small cot. It was nothing like his big bed upstairs, but she knew her brother reveled in being surrounded by Papa's things. It was almost as good as being with Papa. *Almost.*

She waited a moment, hoping Andrew would feel like talking. But all he said was "Good night" and rolled over with his back to Daria. Sometimes she felt as though this horrible war was taking Andrew away from her, too.

Two days before New Year's, a sign painter arrived to create a new sign. The Kevin Fisk, Medical Doctor sign was taken down. In its place hung a sign that said Fisk Boardinghouse—Reasonable Rates.

Daria could hardly bear to see Papa's sign taken down. She tried to remember that she must be strong and a help to Mama.

The new year of 1862 arrived with little fanfare. Cannons were shot in Cincinnati, and other cannons echoed back from across the river at Newport Barracks and Covington. Articles in the newspapers speculated that perhaps this would be the year that ended the war.

The day after New Year's Day, a letter arrived from Papa. Mama took the letter first and closed herself in her room for a time. Daria told Andrew later that she believed that was when Mama allowed herself to cry. "I don't think Mama wants us to know how much she misses Papa and worries about him. She doesn't want us to worry."

The letter was shared as they came together in the parlor late in the evening. Mama read it aloud so they could all hear Papa's description of the camps in Tennessee. He told about the thousands of campfires that were lit each evening and the sad, melancholy singing that floated across the night air:

Hundreds and hundreds of lonely, homesick men and boys all sleeping and eating out in the cold. The rows of tents stretch out as far as the eye can see. Christmas was especially difficult for everyone. To hear "Silent Night" being sung by hundreds of voices all in unison and perfect harmony is enough to break the heart of the most hardened men here.

The men ask over and over, "Why is nothing being done? Why have we all been called out to sit here in the cold and wait?" Morale is low, discouragement high.

Food is another problem. The men have a number of jokes about how terrible it is. "One bean to a gallon of water" is the recipe for the soup. The hardtack biscuits are known as "teeth crackers."

As Mama read that part, Daria thought of the good beef stew she'd just finished for supper, and the light-as-air corn bread that Mirza baked. It wasn't fair that Papa should not be here to share it. The letter continued:

I seem to pray for the men as much as I doctor. Perhaps I'm part chaplain and part doctor.

Many of the boys are ill. I treat many cases of dysentery, typhoid, and flu. Then, of course, there are the fistfights that break out here and there due to the short fuses of some men's tempers. I mend a few broken noses and split lips as well. But as of now, no war wounds. Much as I, too, hate the long wait, I am thankful for that!

Papa closed by giving his love to every one of them. He said nothing about the boardinghouse. Had Mama not told him?

The first boarder arrived three days after the advertisement appeared in the *Gazette*. Daria happened to be at the house when the knock sounded, so she answered the door. There stood a short, stooped man with a thatch of white hair and thick, white chin whiskers. His eyes were gray blue and steely hard. A permanent scowl was etched into his brow. He held his stovepipe hat in his hand. A satchel sat at his feet.

"Good day," Daria said politely. "May I help you?"

"I've come to rent a room," the man said, mumbling his words. That said, he picked up his satchel, moved through the door, and set his satchel down in the hallway as though he owned the place.

So, Daria thought, *this is what it will be like to have boarders.*

CHAPTER 9

Boarders

Daria stared at the stoop-shouldered man, wishing it were possible to order him out of their house. Instead, she waved the man toward the front parlor. "Have a seat, sir. I'll fetch Mama."

Mama was the picture of gracious hospitality as she swept into the parlor and greeted the stranger. Daria waited in the hallway—partly so she could listen and partly to see if Mama might need her.

The man's name was William Martin, and he was a teacher in one of the neighboring school districts. "Thought I was retired from that sort of stuff and nonsense," he told Mama in a low, raspy voice. "But this foolish war has whisked away all our young teachers. So they take us old geezers out of the pasture and put us back to work again. This location will be closer to the school than my room downtown."

"You're the first to answer our advertisement," she told him. "Let me show you the rooms available. You'll have your pick." Her voice was cheery and kind. But Mr. Martin just grunted and got to his feet after a slight struggle. Daria suspected he suffered from rheumatism.

She stepped back out of the way as the two came into the hallway. "I brought a few things with me," Mr. Martin said, holding up his bag. "If I like the place, I'll have the livery bring the rest of my books and clothes later."

"A fine idea," Mama said, still maintaining her cheeriness.

Mr. Martin preferred the guest room that faced the front of the house and paid Mama a deposit.

From the first moment Mr. Martin moved in, he began to complain. This was something entirely new to Mama and Mirza. Papa never complained about anything.

"Who swept my room today?" Mr. Martin asked one evening at supper.

"I did," Daria answered in a meek voice. She was trying hard to follow Mama's example. *I'm helping Mama,* she reminded herself.

"Cobwebs in the corner," Mr. Martin growled between bites. "Even with my failing eyesight, I can see cobwebs in the corner."

Daria glanced at Mama. Mama gave a weak smile and nodded. "I'll be more careful next time," Daria said.

"See that you are," he snapped back.

Fortunately, Mr. Martin spent the evenings in his room grading papers, so the family still had quiet evenings in the parlor. Daria was thankful the old man wasn't her teacher. She wasn't sure she could bear it.

After a week or two of his continual complaining, Daria had had enough. There was only so much a body could stand. Mirza was pouring coffee one morning when Mr. Martin asked, "What did you do to these eggs?"

"Why, I scrambled them, sir," Mirza said.

"Well," he said, not looking up from his plate, "they're terrible. I prefer my eggs just like they come out of the shell. No need beating them all together in a blob."

"Beg your pardon, sir," she said.

Daria could see the look of hurt in her eyes. Then Mirza bolted from the room in tears.

"If you like your eggs as they come out of the shell," Daria retorted, "we'll serve you raw eggs tomorrow morning."

"Daria Ann Fisk!" Mama said with a warning tone to her voice.

"Well, she's right." Andrew stood to his feet. Mr. Martin looked up at him. "When my papa left for the war," Andrew told their boarder, "he told me to look out after this family. And I won't have my mama, my sisters, nor our dear friend Mirza being treated in such a manner. They're ladies and should be treated as ladies."

The room was quiet. Daria had no doubt she and Andrew had just chased off their first and only paying customer.

"You young rascals are all alike," mumbled the old teacher. "Hot-tempered and spoiling for a fight. It's no wonder we're in a war." He wiped his mouth on his napkin, folded it neatly, and said, "I believe I'm nearly late for class." With that, he left the table.

"Daria, Andrew," Mama said softly, "how could you do such a thing? He's old and set in his ways."

"Well, he can learn a few new ways," Daria answered, her heart still hammering in her throat.

"I think they were great, Mama," Jenny said, her eyes gleaming. "I believe Papa would have been proud of them. Mr. William Martin is a bit more irritable than he needs to be, Mama."

"Well, at least he pays his rent each week," Mama said. "That's what's important just now."

Although Mr. Martin never said anything about Daria's and Andrew's outbursts, he stopped complaining as much. Then Mrs. Ryan arrived. Her presence worked to balance things out. The slender, well-dressed lady appeared to be only a few years younger than Mama. Portia Ryan was a lady of means who hailed from Cleveland. Her father and her husband were in business together and owned a packet of canal boats. That is, they had until the war disrupted everything. She told Mama about her officer husband, Ambrose, who lay ill and wounded in the military hospital.

Mrs. Ryan, to Daria's great relief, was the opposite of William Martin. In spite of the fact that she was a paying guest, she was appreciative and offered to pitch in and help with clearing the dishes and preparing the meals. It was a simple matter to clean her room, and Daria didn't mind at all that she had come to stay at the Fisk Boardinghouse.

Mrs. Ryan caught the omnibus each morning to go to the hospital and be with her husband. Mama instructed her to look up Martha Burton, who continued to work at the hospital. "Martha will make sure you have every comfort during your time there," Mama told her.

Before January was over, the family had fallen into a fairly comfortable routine. Daria and Andrew gritted their teeth and performed every job Mama asked of them. But Andrew told Daria he prayed no boys from his class ever came by while he was outside shaking rugs!

Before going to sleep each night, Daria and Andrew spent time in the stable with Bordeaux. Afterward, Andrew would go to his room, open the window and whistle, then call out softly, "Good night, Bordeaux. Good night, boy." Bordeaux would thrust his head out of the window of his stall and nicker his reply. Daria couldn't help but feel jealous. She was getting used to sharing a room with Jenny—but she would rather have had Bordeaux nearby the way Andrew did.

One Friday night, Daria and Andrew sat on his cot, whispering until the house was quiet around them. Daria was relieved to share her thoughts with Andrew the way they always used to, but she realized that Andrew wasn't telling her as much as she was telling him. She fell silent, hoping he would take the opportunity to talk. Then, in the midst of the silence, both children heard noises outside the door. They turned toward each other, holding their breath.

There it was again. Noises right at the door. A sliver of moon hung in the sky, giving a little light, and Daria could see a shadow moving.

"Is it a burglar?" she whispered, her heart pounding. She'd read in the paper about desperate people who'd been financially ruined by the war. They were ready to steal in order to survive.

She watched as Andrew slowly crawled out of bed and crept over to the stove. He picked up the poker. Grasping the cold metal rod in his hand, he froze as the noise sounded one more time. This time the knob rattled.

Raising the poker above his head, Andrew stepped cautiously toward the door. He placed his hand on the glass knob, ready to yank it open and bring down the poker on whoever was out there. "Be careful," Daria breathed. Holding his breath, Andrew turned the knob and yanked it open.

Daria let out a gasp that was half scream, half giggle. Her brother had only just stopped himself from giving Bordeaux a crowning blow with the poker. The huge hulk of a horse stood with his nose right at the door.

Andrew burst out laughing. "Bordeaux, you scared me plum out of a year's growth." Dropping the poker, he reached out to pet the sleek neck. "You silly old piece of horseflesh. Do you know how close you came to getting a hard conk on the noggin? Do you?"

Daria couldn't stop laughing. "How in the world did he get out?" she managed to say between giggles. "Did we leave that door open?"

"Wait just a minute till I get some warm clothes on," Andrew said, "and I'll go check." Leaving the door ajar, he went back in to pull on his coat and slip his bare feet into his shoes. When he turned around again, the front half of Bordeaux's body was inside the door. Daria was giggling even harder now.

"Hey, you silly thing. You can't come in here, much as I'd like to have your company." He put his hand on Bordeaux's white blaze forehead and pushed him back. "Out with you now. I have no hay or oats for you in here."

There was no halter or bridle, but none was needed. Daria watched from the window as Bordeaux followed beside Andrew like a puppy as the two of them strolled through the cold January night back to the stable. She sucked in her breath when she realized the doors to the stable and stall were standing open. Daria was sure they'd closed them. They always closed them. She snatched up one of Andrew's quilts, wrapped it around her shoulders, and dashed out to the stable.

"How did the doors get open?" she asked her brother.

Andrew looked up at the horse and asked him, "Did you do this?" Andrew moved the sliding wooden bolt back and forth. Bordeaux nodded.

In the dim moonlight, Daria looked up at the kind brown eyes. "You are one incredible horse," she whispered. "You truly are." The children put their arms around the great neck.

Daria heard her brother whisper to the horse, "You miss Papa, too, don't you?"

Children and beast stood quietly for a moment, as though their presence soothed each other. Daria wished she could always feel this close to Andrew.

At last, Andrew sighed and stepped back. "You can't be out roaming around," he told Bordeaux as he put the horse back into the stall. "Someone might steal you away. You can't trust anyone these days. Especially with Rebel spies roaming the city." He closed the stall door and shoved a little stick into the hole so the bolt wouldn't slide.

The next morning at breakfast, Andrew told the others how Bordeaux had opened the doors in the stable.

Mr. Martin just snorted. "You probably left them open. Just like a young striplin' like you to do that and then blame it on a dumb animal."

"Bordeaux is not a dumb animal," Daria protested. Mama gave her a look.

"Horses are smart," Mrs. Ryan put in, smiling kindly at Daria and Andrew. "Very smart. God gave them a wonderful sense that humans know very little about."

That morning it was Daria's turn to do the job she hated most—serve breakfast. "Our uncle Jon trained Bordeaux and raised him from a foal." She set the platter of ham and eggs on the table. "He and Aunt Ellie give their horses tender love and affection."

Mrs. Ryan nodded. "My Ambrose says if you treat a horse right, it'll save your life if need be."

"I think," Jenny said to Andrew and Daria, "that Bordeaux wants you to know he understands how you feel."

Another grunt came from Mr. Martin. "You been feeding him apples. I've seen you two. He was just wanting another apple."

But it didn't matter what Mr. Martin said. Andrew and Daria knew better. Daria glanced over at Mama. There were tears in her eyes. Mama knew, too.

The third room was empty for a time, then filled, then empty again. Mama thought perhaps Jenny could move back into her own room again, since they didn't seem to have any more nibbles. But Jenny said she was fine and that they should wait awhile longer. The two girls had learned to take comfort from each other's presence at night. And the rent paid by Mrs. Ryan and Mr. Martin was helping the budget a great deal.

The first week in February brought another letter from Roy. He was still with the Army of the Potomac. Just as Daria had suspected, Roy had spent a miserable Christmas in the cold, eating terrible military food. The letter was fairly short.

We don't do nothing but eat, sleep, and drill. While I don't mean to talk bad about a friend of your fokes, I have to say slo-poke McClellan is making the war stretch out intolerably long. We was all feeling hepped up about how many troops he has brought together. But for what? We just set and set and set. I hear tell even Old Abe is mad at him.

In spite of all, I do tolerably well. The soljers here say I'm a right good drummer. It stays awful cold.

Tell Daria I'm learning more to pray. The chaplin here is helping me.

Yore fren, Roy

At twilight a few days after Roy's letter arrived, Andrew and Daria were in the stable taking care of the tack. Knowing how fussy Papa was about the harnesses, they were determined to keep them ready, just as though Papa might be coming home any day.

Cold, gray rain had been drizzling down most of the day. Daria figured it would turn to sleet or snow by morning. Suddenly, church bells began tolling loudly throughout the city. Her heart sped up.

Mama came out the side door from the kitchen. "Children? You hear that?"

"Yes'm, I sure do," Andrew said. "Want us to go see about it?"

"We'd all be obliged." She stepped quickly back inside to get out of the chill.

Andrew saddled Bordeaux, Daria scrambled up behind him, and they headed for town. In spite of the nasty weather, a crowd had clustered around the office of the *Gazette*. People were saying something about Fort Henry.

The children dismounted, and Andrew led Bordeaux through the crowd. "What is it?" he asked an older man. "What's happened?"

"Happened? Grant's just taken Fort Henry, with nary a shot fired; that's what happened! It's a pure miracle. That's what it is!"

Daria knew from her maps at school that Fort Henry was in Tennessee on the Tennessee River. This was an important victory. It was good to ride home to tell Mama and Jenny the good news.

But less than a week later, the news wasn't quite so heartening. Less than eleven miles from Fort Henry, on the Cumberland River, was Fort Donelson. The officer holding the fort surrendered it to Ulysses S. Grant, but only after many lives had been lost. Daria knew Papa was in Tennessee. She tried to imagine how difficult it would be to care for so many wounded men.

The paper reported that when the commander of the fort asked about surrender conditions, Grant sent back the message that nothing less than unconditional surrender would be accepted. Relieved that someone in the Union army was ready to fight, the citizens of Cincinnati began to cheer for "Unconditional Surrender" Grant.

"God bless Grant!" the crowd cried. The bells rang long into the night hours. With both of the forts in Union hands, the way was clear to move in and take Nashville, the capital of Tennessee. Surely this news meant the war was nearly over.

Daria worried a great deal about Papa's safety. Nearly three thousand men were dead, wounded, or missing after that terrible battle. And the paper said the Confederate losses were much greater. She could not imagine that much death and dying all in one place.

On a Saturday late in February, Mama had them all cleaning the house. Mama had turned almost every Saturday into a cleaning day ever since their home became a boardinghouse. There was plenty of scrubbing and sweeping. Daria could never remember Mama doing so much cleaning.

The air was still chilly, but the sting of winter was beginning to wane. Mama decided the porch needed a scrubbing, so that's where Daria was when she saw a young man walking up to the house. Not walking exactly. Limping was more like it. He was dressed in a rumpled blue uniform with corporal insignias, and he leaned heavily on a cane as he walked.

Daria sat back on her heels and stared as the man approached. He came right up to the porch steps. He was not very tall, but he had a broad chest like he'd chopped trees or rowed boats all his life. He politely removed his hat, displaying his long, wavy chestnut hair. It was the same color as his mustache.

Nodding toward the sign, the young man asked, "This here the Fisk residence? Family of Dr. Kevin Fisk, captain in the Union forces?"

"Yes, sir, it is. My papa is with Grant's men in Tennessee."

"I know."

"You know?"

"He helped treat my leg. I just wanted to stop and pay my regards."

Daria jumped to her feet, nearly knocking over her bucket of scrub water. Sticking her head in the door, she shouted, "Mama! Mama! Come quick. Here's a man who's been with Papa!"

CHAPTER 10

Corporal Philip Harnden

At Daria's call, Mama came running to the door, wiping her hands on her apron. She stepped out onto the porch and extended her hand to the stranger.

"Welcome, Corporal," she said. "I'm Mrs. Fisk, Pamela Fisk. This is my daughter Daria."

The corporal had to place his hat in the hand holding the cane before accepting her handshake. "My pleasure, Mrs. Fisk. I'm Corporal Philip Harnden." Then he reached over to shake Daria's hand, as well. "Daria. Pleased to meet you."

The hand was strong and the grasp firm. The brown eyes were lively, and the mouth seemed accustomed to a smile. Some of the wounded that Daria had seen come back to town had empty, sad eyes. But not this man.

"Please do come in." Mama held the door to let him go in, but he stepped back.

"After you, ma'am."

"Thank you," Mama answered. Daria could tell she was pleased at his manners.

"Daria, you take the corporal into the parlor. I'll have Mirza fix tea." Turning to the corporal, she added, "You'll have to excuse our appearance. We've been cleaning."

"No apologies necessary, ma'am," he told her.

"My other daughter and my son are upstairs working. I'll call them down, as well."

Daria had never seen Mama so flustered.

"That would be nice," the corporal said, his eyes crinkling at the corners when he smiled.

As Mama left, Daria directed the visitor into the parlor. "Make yourself comfortable," she said.

Corporal Harnden entered the room. He paused, leaned on his cane, and looked around. "Hmm. Nice." He pointed to Papa's chair nearest the fireplace. "I'm sure that's Captain Fisk's chair."

"Yes, it is. We'd be honored to have you sit there," Daria told him. She surprised herself by saying it. The chair was so special now. Only Mama sat there when they had their prayers each evening.

"I wouldn't think of it," the corporal said. He limped over to the settee and lowered himself onto it gingerly.

"Is Papa all right?" Daria asked. "When did you see him last? Were you at Fort Donelson?"

Philip Harnden laughed. "Hey there. Not so fast. No sense in repeating myself. Your mama, sister, and brother will have the same questions."

Just then, Andrew came flying in through the door. His face was smudged with dirt from cleaning the stoves upstairs, and his hair stuck out every which way. Jenny was right on his heels, looking not much better.

The corporal struggled to get up, but Andrew came nearer and said, "Please don't get up." He looked at the cane. "I'm Andrew, Daria's twin. And this is my older sister, Mrs. Edward Stephens. Her husband is with McClellan back in Virginia."

Corporal Harnden politely shook hands with both of them while remaining seated. Waving toward the leg, he said, "This is so new, I've not quite grown accustomed yet to being crippled."

Jenny put her hand to her mouth. "Is it bad?"

"I'm alive," said the corporal, "and I still have the leg. That's all that matters just now."

Mama and Mirza came in carrying trays with things for tea. Jenny rose quickly to lend a hand. "Please sit down, Mama. Let me do this."

Daria eyed the little iced cakes. They must have been intended for supper. Mirza could still create miracles in the kitchen in spite of the sugar shortage.

Mama did as Jenny asked, sitting down in Papa's chair. After tea had been served, Mama said, "Please, Corporal, tell us about Dr. Fisk. Is he well? Did he ask you to come see us? Did you bring a letter?"

"Your questions are as numerous as your young daughter's," the corporal said with a smile. "No, he did not send me. In fact, he probably doesn't even remember me. There were so many wounded at Donelson."

"You were in the fighting at Fort Donelson?" Andrew asked. Daria knew how bloody that place had been. It had been so cold that many of the wounded simply lay on the ground and froze to death.

"I was. And your father and the other doctors—there were so few—treated the wounded with extreme compassion. I was just one of many whom he treated. I also observed him interacting with the men in camp. He's a fine man. You can be proud of him."

"How did you happen to come by?" Jenny wanted to know. "I mean, if Papa didn't send you."

The corporal accepted another cake from Daria before answering. "It was a bit of a coincidence. I'm passing through on my way back to my home in Chicago—that is, I think I'm going there. When I arrived in town, I remembered that Captain Fisk said he was from this city, so I just asked around to find where he lived. It wasn't difficult to find the home of a beloved doctor."

"Why did you say you *think* you're going back to Chicago?"

Mama asked. "Aren't you sure?"

"Actually, ma'am, I'm not sure at all. When I was first hurt, I felt that was the only alternative. But I have no family there. My parents and sister died of cholera a few years ago."

"I'm so sorry," Mama said.

"Thank you, ma'am," he said. "But aside from having no family there, it seems far from the war and what's happening. You see, each day my leg's improving. Now I'm wondering if I might remain close to the war and rejoin my unit when I'm able."

"You'd go back and fight again?" Daria asked.

"That I would," he said.

Daria admired this man's courage. What a dynamic soldier he must be. If he hadn't been wounded, the man would have gone right up in rank. She turned to look at her twin, and she knew he was thinking the same thing she was.

"What about our extra room?" Andrew asked.

Mama looked at him. *He's probably spoken out of turn,* Daria thought, holding her breath for their mama's reply.

"Extra room?" the corporal asked. "I saw your sign, but in this busy city, I assumed all your rooms would be taken."

"Oddly enough, the one room has gone begging for a number of weeks," Mama told him. "Would you care to take a look?"

The corporal smiled. "Even as I was riding the omnibus out here from town, I kept asking over and over what I should do with myself during this time. Now it seems God has answered my prayers."

A soldier right in their house! Daria could hardly believe their good fortune. She would feel even more as though she was actually helping the war effort. She'd also feel closer to Papa by having this man in their midst.

Daria jumped up. "May I show him upstairs, Mama? May I, please?"

"We just finished cleaning in there," Jenny said. "The rugs aren't back down yet, but it's presentable."

"But the corporal's not even finished with his tea," Mama said. "Don't rush him."

"Yes, I am." He upended the dainty cup, downing the last of the tea, and set it back on the saucer. "And it was delicious. I can't tell you how long it's been since I enjoyed such a pleasant teatime." Scooting forward on the settee, he firmed the cane to support his weight before carefully standing to his feet.

Suddenly, Daria realized they were all staring at him as he struggled to get to his feet. She gave her brother a nudge, and he rushed forward. "May I give you a hand?" he offered awkwardly.

"You're very kind, but I've been trying my best to learn to do everything on my own."

Daria understood. She was sure she'd be the same way. She wouldn't want to be treated like a cripple. Then she wondered about the stairs. How would the corporal manage? Should she say something?

But when the corporal reached the stairway that led up from the front hall, he looked at them and said, "What excellent exercise this will be for a game leg."

Daria was amazed at his attitude. "Right this way," she said, leading the way up the steps.

Daria could tell that the corporal liked the room. He limped about the room touching things, sat on the bed, and then bounced a couple times. "Was this your room?"

Daria shook her head. "Jenny's. My room is where Mrs. Ryan is staying. Her husband is at the military hospital. She's from Cleveland."

"An officer?"

"A lieutenant."

"Any other boarders?"

Daria screwed up her face. "An old man—a teacher named William Martin."

"You don't care for this Mr. Martin, I take it."

"He's mean as an old polecat with a thorn in his paw."

The corporal smiled. "Sometimes older folk are in a good deal of pain. Instead of telling you about the pain, they complain about everything else. Helps them let off a little steam, so to speak."

Daria had never thought about that. Mr. Martin did move about with a great deal of difficulty. "Will your pain make you irritable, as well?" she asked.

"I'm not sure yet. It's too new to tell. I'm hoping the pain will be gone before I have a chance to fall into that trap."

"I spoke sharply to Mr. Martin one morning when he made Mirza cry, but it didn't do any good."

"Too set in his ways to change, probably."

The corporal looked up and smiled as Andrew came into the room. "Tell me, Andrew," he said, "since you gave up your room, where did your mother put you? In the attic?"

"I sleep in Papa's office—in the waiting room. We borrowed a cot."

"That's a big sacrifice for a young man to make—to give up his room. And I'd be willing to guess you also help with all the work around here, cleaning and so on. That, too, is a big sacrifice for children your age."

The corporal was looking out the windows at the carriage house in the back. "And you have horses?" Bordeaux's proud head could be seen through the open stable window.

"Horse," Daria answered. "Only one. Bordeaux is Papa's horse to pull his buggy. But Andrew and I are taking care of him in Papa's absence."

"A French name for a horse?"

"My aunt is of French descent, so she likes to give their horses

French names. Bordeaux came from their stables."

"And who might your aunt be?"

"Eleanor Burton—"

"Wife of Jonathan Burton, the attorney?"

Daria perked up. "You've heard of my uncle?"

"Hasn't everyone? A close associate of our secretary of treasury, Salmon Chase, and also well known for his work in defending runaway slaves before the war."

Daria was impressed. She hadn't really thought of people knowing her uncle's name. He was just Uncle Jon to Daria.

"Uncle Jon is Mama's brother," Andrew explained, "and he comes over to check on us regularly since Papa's been away. Perhaps you'll meet him while you're staying with us. That is, if you decide to take the room."

"I'd like to meet your uncle," the corporal replied. "And I do believe I've decided to take the room."

Daria felt her heart skip a beat. She hadn't been this excited since the war started last April. "Good. That's good, Corporal. Will you be staying right this minute? I mean, you can. The room's all clean."

The corporal's eyes crinkled again. "First of all, since I'm not now in active service, let's dispense with the corporal business. I'm just plain old Philip to you. Agreed?"

"All right, Philip." It seemed strange to Daria since the man was in uniform.

"And next, my things are downtown at the hotel. I still have a little business to take care of in town, so I'll come out tomorrow afternoon after church."

"Come in time for Sunday dinner. You can't imagine what a good cook Mirza is," Andrew insisted. "In fact, I'll have the buggy all hitched up to take Mama and my sisters to church. I can come to get you myself after I bring them home."

But Philip raised his hand to protest. "I wouldn't dream of putting you out. I'll take the omnibus. I have only a couple of small satchels—no need for curb service with the family buggy."

Andrew blushed. Daria knew he was afraid he'd been too forward. "Well, then," he said awkwardly, "I guess we can go down and tell Mama the room is now taken."

CHAPTER 11

A Friend Named Philip

Philip Harnden's arrival at the Fisk home seemed to change everything. The man was friendly and cheerful, with a good disposition. He could talk about almost anything, yet he never did so in an arrogant manner. He had a way of sharing things that made them interesting.

Like Mrs. Ryan, he wanted to lend a hand every chance he got. The first Sunday night he was there, he surprised them all by helping Mirza bring things to the table at supper. He grabbed a platter of roast beef, and leaning on his cane with one hand, he maneuvered through the swinging door from the kitchen into the dining room.

"Now there, Corporal," Mirza said, "you needn't do that."

"She's right," Mama said. "Please don't bother. You're the paying customer in this place."

"But I enjoy helping," he told her. "The more I can do and the more confident I become, the sooner I'll be fully well."

Daria had never heard of a man who wanted to do women's work. After dinner, Philip helped to gather up the dirty plates and carry them to the kitchen.

With a smile on her face, Mirza said to Mama, "I believe we ought to pay him to stay with us." They all chuckled. Daria had to admit that it felt good to have something to laugh about.

With Philip around, it never mattered to anyone what Mr. Martin said about the food being bad, or the bed being too lumpy, or the room being too cold. Philip was appreciative and grateful for each and every little thing.

"Once you've slept on the frozen ground or marched for miles in dust or mud on an empty stomach, you learn to be thankful," he told them.

But then when he saw Jenny's face go pale, he apologized. "I didn't mean to bring up unpleasant subjects," he told her. "Or for you, either, ma'am," he added, turning to Mama.

"You can't help but talk of what you've experienced," Mama told him. "We don't fault you for that. You've already brought us pleasure by speaking kindly of Dr. Fisk. We're certainly aware that war is an unpleasant experience."

The first few days, Philip spent most of his time resting in his room. He'd located a bookstore and the library, and he made periodic trips to both places, keeping himself stocked with a good supply of books. Daria learned almost immediately that Philip Harnden loved to read.

One evening toward the end of the first week, Philip asked if he might join Andrew and Daria in bedding down Bordeaux for the night. "I've seen that big fellow from a distance. I'd like to have a closer look."

"We'd be pleased to have your company," Daria replied.

"Be back inside in time for prayers, children," Mama chided.

"Yes, ma'am." When they were outside, Daria told Philip, "Ever since Papa's been gone, Mama's real strict about prayers and stuff like that."

"And how fortunate for you that she is. She takes her responsibility for her family very seriously."

They'd gone out the front way and were walking slowly around the side of the house. While the late February evening was still quite chilly, there'd been no more snow for a time. Daria and Andrew consciously slowed their pace to match Philip's limp.

"Your mother's very proud of both of you, you know," Philip told them.

Daria felt her face grow warm. Of course, she knew Mama loved her, but she'd not thought about Mama being proud of her. And Andrew knew how disappointed Mama was about his grades. Since the children didn't know how to answer the corporal, neither of them said anything.

Philip was immensely impressed with Bordeaux. "This is about the finest horse I've seen anywhere," he told Daria and Andrew. "And I've seen a lot of horses in my day."

"Uncle Jon is almost as well known for his horses as he is for his work with Salmon Chase," Daria said proudly, running her hand along Bordeaux's strong back.

Reaching up to stroke Bordeaux's nose, Philip said, "If Bordeaux is typical of the breeding lines, I'm not surprised. What's the wire for?" he asked, pointing to the stall door.

Andrew smiled. Jabbing a thumb toward the door to Papa's office, he said, "After I moved downstairs, I started opening the window to call good night to him. Since he knew where I was, he decided to come calling."

Philip laughed a nice deep laugh that came right up out of his big chest. "He learned how to slip the bolt back?"

"He did. The first time it happened, Mr. Martin accused me of leaving the doors open. But I know I closed them. So the next time, I put a stick in the latch, and he chewed the stick right off and opened it again. Now I have to wire it." Andrew reached up to slap Bordeaux gently on his side. "I guess if I didn't, he'd open the office door and come in and sleep with me."

Philip laughed again, which made Daria and Andrew laugh, as well.

"Mrs. Ryan told us," Daria went on, "that her husband says if you treat a horse right, he might well save your life sometime."

"It's been known to happen, especially on the battlefield."

Daria opened the stall door, brought Bordeaux out, and fastened him with the cross ties. Andrew opened the tack box, grabbed a brush, and handed a currycomb to Philip. Bordeaux stood still as Philip and Andrew moved to either side of the big animal and began grooming. Daria stroked Bordeaux's soft nose.

"I've seen hardened soldiers weep over the death of a good horse," Philip said. "They grieve over the loss of a horse almost as much as over the death of a comrade."

Daria could believe that. It would be a terrible thing if they ever lost Bordeaux. Andrew and Philip worked together in silence for a time, and then Philip said, "Where do you like to ride?"

"Mostly we just go into town to the *Gazette* to bring back the war news for Mama."

"If you took a long ride, where would you go?"

"Probably out to the fairgrounds—I mean, to Camp Harrison," Andrew said. "It used to be the fairgrounds. It's shady along the way and a pleasant ride. Sometimes we ride to the cabin where our older brother Christian lives. It's near the Little Miami Railroad on the east side of town. You've not met Christian yet. He works for the railroad."

"How about if I rent a mount from the livery and the three of us take a ride together some Saturday? That is, if my game leg will allow me to do such things."

Daria looked around the back of Bordeaux to see the man's face. Surely he was joshing. Why would this army corporal want to spend time with two twelve-year-olds? But Philip Harnden wasn't joshing. "I'd like that, Philip," Daria said. "I'd like that a lot."

Andrew took the pick and carefully cleaned Bordeaux's hooves and checked his shoes, while Philip untangled the mane and forelock and Daria combed his tail. When they were finished, Philip asked, "Do you think Mrs. Fisk would mind if I sat in on your family prayer time this evening?"

Daria closed the stall door and fastened it tightly with the wire. "She wouldn't mind. You already seem like one of the family." Daria smiled as she said the words. It really did seem like Philip Harnden belonged.

Mr. Martin was now the only person in the Fisk Boardinghouse who never lifted a finger to help. Having both Philip and Mrs. Ryan as boarders made things easier, because their rooms were always neat and because they enjoyed lending a hand, even when it was time to clean. Over Mama's protests, of course.

As March warmth began to chase winter's barrenness from the air, Mama's countenance changed. The worry lines were vanishing.

When she sat at her secretary to work on the account books, she came away with a smile on her face. Daria had to admit, her mother's decision to open a boardinghouse had been wise.

One gloriously sunny Saturday after the cleaning was finished, Daria and Andrew asked their mother if they could go riding with the corporal. "But, Andrew, we have to do the repairs you promised you would help me with today."

Andrew sighed and nodded. "Daria," Mama continued, "why don't you and Philip go for a ride? It'll be all right. Andrew can join you when we finish."

Philip went to the livery to rent a mount. "Slim pickings," he told Daria with a laugh when he returned with the horse. Daria had to agree. The horse's coat was dull. His bearing was saggy and his manner listless. "All the good horses have gone to war, just as all the good men have," Philip joked.

"Where shall we go?" Daria asked as she saddled Bordeaux.

"I should like to meet your brother, Christian. Let's head out in that direction."

"He may not be there," Daria warned. "We never know if he's away with a train or home between trips."

"The ride will be enjoyable either way."

"I'll take you through the hills," Daria said as she mounted Bordeaux. "Christian's cabin is at the edge of town."

It was a perfect day to be out, and Daria was thankful, too, for the sense of hope Philip seemed to have given the entire family. She breathed deeply of the spring air and was lulled by the gentle squeaking of the leather saddle and clopping of the hooves. She led the way through the sparser neighborhoods on Mount Auburn and Mount Adams.

"How's your leg faring?" she asked as they came through a cool stand of trees at the foot of Mount Adams. She'd noticed that Philip stuck his cane through the loops on the saddle so he'd have it handy.

"I wasn't sure at first how riding would affect it, but it's not too bad. Nothing I can't tolerate."

Philip never said too much about the leg, and Daria wondered if he were in pain much of the time. The man never complained.

"How's school?" Philip asked.

Daria smiled. "I don't mind school so much, but I would rather be helping with the war effort."

"What's your favorite subject?"

"I love to read. I read almost anything I can get my hands on."

"I didn't like school for a long time," Philip confessed.

"You didn't?"

"I surely did not."

Daria was always surprised when someone told her they did not like school. And yet she knew how much her twin hated the classroom. Maybe there was hope for Andrew yet, if Philip, too, had had trouble in school. "What did you do about it?"

"A kindly teacher got me interested in reading. 'Books,' she said to me, 'are our windows to the world.' At first I didn't believe her. But she was patient with me."

"I don't remember never liking to read. But Andrew—he has a lot of problems with reading."

"Maybe I can help him."

Daria pulled Bordeaux to a stop and let Philip's weaker horse catch up. "Do you think you could? He knows that Mama and Papa are disappointed when he doesn't get good marks, and it makes Andrew so sad. I try to help him, but. . ." How could she explain the walls that had risen between her and her brother?

Philip smiled, his eyes crinkling at the corners. "If he gives me a chance. And gives himself a chance. Think he could do that?"

A wounded corporal wanted to take the time to help Andrew. Daria felt confident. "If you're willing, Andrew would be a dunce to refuse."

They had reached a creek in a wooded area at the edge of town, and they let their horses stop for a drink. From there, it was only a short distance to Christian's old cabin.

"There it is." Daria pointed. "That's where Christian lives."

The cabin was made of squared logs with a rock chimney at one end. The area around it was cross-fenced. Several horses grazed in one of the corrals.

"Smoke's coming from the chimney. That means someone's there," Daria said.

As they approached, the front door of the cabin opened. There stood Christian. "Hey there, Daria. What's going on? Welcome!"

"Christian! I have someone I want you to meet." Quickly Daria slid out of the saddle. She wondered if Philip needed assistance, but she didn't know how to offer help without embarrassing the man. But Philip slid off, landed on his good leg, and quickly grabbed the cane to steady himself. Daria reached over and took the reins and hitched both horses to the rail out front.

"Christian, I'd like you to meet our newest boarder, Corporal Philip Harnden. He was with Papa at Fort Donelson."

Daria could tell from Christian's expression that he was pleased by this. "You've seen Captain Fisk?"

The two shook hands as Philip said, "That I have. He's a good man and a fine doctor."

Christian led the way inside the cabin. It was dim inside and mostly in a state of disarray. Not much of Mama's teachings on cleanliness seemed to have rubbed off on Christian. But then, two other railroad men lived there, as well. A rough-hewn table sat in the middle of the room with two cots off to the side. A straight ladder led to the loft, where the third bed was located. On another wall, wooden shelves held Christian's books.

"Lucky for you I got coffee on," Christian told them. He fetched three tin cups and proceeded to fill them from the pot on the wood-burning stove. After Christian sat down, he asked Philip a number of questions about Tennessee and the fighting there.

"I never go that way," Christian told him, "and the newspapers back East act like that area doesn't exist. All they write about is the Army of the Potomac."

Then it was Philip's turn to ask questions. "So what's McClellan planning now that the winter is over?"

Christian shook his head. "No one knows. I don't think the president even knows. But most people are getting pretty impatient to have something happen to get this war over with."

"I've heard the number of troops Lincoln has amassed. Are there really that many? And where are they all?"

Christian went to his bureau and came back with a piece of brown wrapping paper and the stub of a pencil. He drew lines and diagrams, explaining where all the troops were deployed. As Daria listened and sipped the bitter coffee, she wondered which little part of that map marked Roy's whereabouts.

Christian and Philip seemed to take to one another just fine, and this made Daria even more pleased. Christian told a few tales that Daria knew he would never tell in Mama's presence for fear of worrying her. For instance, Christian explained how the engineers had lined their cabins with boilerplate to protect themselves from the bullets of Rebel snipers. One time, they nearly ran into a stretch of tracks where Rebels had torn up the rails.

"If we'd hit it, I probably wouldn't be sitting here telling about it," Christian said matter-of-factly.

As she sat there listening, Daria suddenly realized that her brother was a war hero just as much as those who carried guns into battle. She couldn't wait to tell Andrew.

The afternoon sped by as the two men swapped stories by the dozens. All too soon it was time to leave. As they rode back into town a different way, Daria suggested they go to the livery to return Philip's mount and then ride home double on Bordeaux.

It didn't seem right to have Philip sit on the rump behind her, so Daria offered the saddle to Philip and hoisted herself up on the back. She never thought she'd want another person to be in control of Papa's horse. But with Philip, it just seemed right.

All the way home from the livery stable, Philip joked about the difference between the old nag from the livery and the regal Bordeaux.

One afternoon, a week after the visit with Christian, Daria went into Philip's room to do the sweeping. Philip, Mama had told her, was downtown at the bookstore for the day. Daria took up the rugs, placed them out in the hall, and began sweeping the floor. Suddenly, a book on the bureau caught her eye. She dropped the broom and went to pick it up. On the cover were the words *Base Ball Guidebook* by Henry Chadwick.

"A book," she whispered. "A book about baseball!"

CHAPTER 12

Baseball Returns

When Philip arrived home just before supper, Daria ran out to the omnibus to greet him. "I wasn't snooping, but I couldn't help noticing you have a book about baseball in your room. Do you like baseball?"

"I love the game," Philip said. "Played it all the time back in Chicago before the war."

Daria felt a surge of excitement race through her. "We have a ball and bat!"

"Well, fancy that." Philip leaned heavily on his cane as he made his way up the front walk. "You ever heard of Chadwick—the man who wrote that book?"

"Never."

"He's chairman of the National Association of Baseball Players in New York. Men on the teams there call him Father Chadwick. He's been writing about baseball for the *New York Clipper* for a number of years now. Somewhere in my things, I have a few clippings of those writings."

Daria could hardly believe what she was hearing. For all these months, baseball had been totally lost to her. She had worried that by the time the war was over and people had time for baseball again, she would be too old to play. Lately, Mama had stopped talking about Daria having to act like a young lady, but Daria knew her reprieve would be temporary. Sooner or later, she would have to grow up. But maybe, just maybe, she'd have the chance to play baseball again first.

101

"Seems to me," Philip said, "we've found a good book to begin a little project."

"What do you mean?" Andrew had joined them, and now he hopped up the stairs of the porch and opened the door to let Philip come through. Philip took off his hat and hung it on the hall tree. He gave Daria a wink.

"How about we make a deal, Andrew? You read the book by Chadwick, and then we'll play some ball." He looked down at his leg as though he wanted to curse it. "Well, what I mean is, we'll play as much as I can. And I can give you plenty of pointers. How's that?"

Andrew grinned. "A right fair deal, sir."

"Then we'll progress from there to another book, a few more ball practices, another book, and a few more practices."

"Sort of like earning the practices by reading a book?"

"Precisely." Philip gave Daria another wink, and she grinned back at him. Not only was she going to get to play baseball again, but Philip had found a way to help Andrew with his reading at the same time.

Daria smiled as she watched the way Andrew could hardly wait until all the chores were done, Bordeaux was taken care of for the night, and prayer time was over. She knew he was eager to start on the book. Imagine, her brother actually wanted to read a book!

After a couple of days, Andrew had finished the entire book, and they were ready to start playing. Philip decided that he would use a crutch during their playing times. That way his hands would be free for catching the ball. They devised a practice area between the apple orchard and the carriage house. Daria hadn't been this happy since before the guns first fired at Fort Sumter almost a year ago.

News from the war early in April told of a terrible battle near a little Methodist church in Tennessee called Shiloh. The Confederates under General Albert S. Johnston attacked General Grant's lines at Pittsburgh Landing. After an initial success on the part of the Confederates, they were finally driven back.

Mrs. Voorhees pointed out the places on the map at school. Though it seemed a small victory, with thousands of lives lost, still it meant more than one hundred miles of the Mississippi River had been taken over by the Union forces. It was difficult to cheer for the victories, though, when so many were dead and wounded.

Nearly every moment of every day, Daria wondered about Papa—where he was and what he was doing and if he was still safe.

Following the battle at Shiloh, hundreds of wounded began streaming into the hospitals in Cincinnati. Many of the women were asked to help care for the soldiers. Mama and Jenny shifted their work from the sewing circle to helping out at the hospitals. After working all day with the wounded men, they were always very quiet.

Toward the close of April, the bells across the city pealed for hours as more good news arrived. Commander David Glasgow Farragut had taken the city of New Orleans. Andrew purchased several papers, and at the supper table that evening, Philip read bits and pieces of the news aloud to everyone. Farragut was a Southerner by birth, yet he had chosen to defend the Union.

The paper explained that Farragut had a fleet of seventeen ships with which he had created a blockade across the mouth of the Mississippi. When Farragut learned that the Union forces were at Vicksburg, he determined to take New Orleans, which was seventy miles upriver. To get there, he had to take his fleet past heavily armed Confederate forts. But the brave commander did what he set out to do—he took New Orleans. It was a great day.

A letter from Papa, which arrived many weeks after Shiloh, told bits and pieces of how terrible that battle had been. When a letter from Papa came, Mama first read it alone. Then the family gathered in private in the parlor to read it together. As Mama read the letter aloud, they knew Papa wasn't telling a fraction of the details of the bloody battle. Instead, he wrote of the lovely peach orchard that had been in full bloom before the battle:

> *Such a small thing it was, to have the lovely trees destroyed, and yet it saddened me to see the pretty blossoms shredded to bits along with all the dear young men.*

Papa also told how in March, while General Grant was inspecting the lines in the rain, his horse fell and pinned the general's leg. Papa had been the one to tend to the general's swelling ankle.

> *We hear out here that newspapers back East are speaking disparagingly about Grant. But know this from me; he is a fine man and a sterling leader. I would take one Grant over ten McClellans any day.*

Mama looked at each of them. Mary Ellen was Mama's dear friend, but they knew Papa would never say such a thing unless he truly believed it. Papa never gossiped.

"Never let that statement go any further than this room," Mama instructed them firmly. "Poor Mary Ellen has enough grief without our adding to it in any way."

In spite of the war, that spring was filled with a number of good things. Philip was invited to several teas about town, where Mama introduced him to Lucy Hayes and Mary Ellen McClellan, as well as to Uncle Jon and Aunt Ellie. In May, Philip decided to take a clerk job at the bookstore to occupy his spare time. Then he joined a literary club that met in the back room of the bookstore.

The glamour of war seemed to have lessened its grip on the boys at school. As the war progressed, fewer boys remained. When the weather grew warmer, Daria and Andrew were able to organize a few children to at least make a semblance of a ball team. Recess was fun again.

Daria was glad to see that Andrew was enjoying himself again. She could see that the past year had brought changes to both of them, but the changes in Andrew had bothered her almost more than the changes in herself. She was proud of her brother, though, because he seemed perfectly content to do "women's work." He thought nothing of serving food to their boarders, washing up the dishes, emptying the chamber pots, or shaking out rugs.

As the end of school drew near, Andrew's marks had made a definite turnaround. They were still not as good as Daria's, but they were much better than the failing marks he'd had before. Daria and Philip confessed to her mother that they had planned the "tutoring."

"I must admit that I am very happy with Andrew's progress," Mama remarked.

Philip continued to bring books to Andrew. At first Philip made every effort to bring books he knew would interest Andrew, but as their project progressed, he occasionally slipped in a book of essays or poetry.

When Andrew wrinkled up his nose at them, Philip just laughed. "This is a new step in our project," he explained. "For every book you read because you like the topic, you must read something in which you have no knowledge or interest. This is how you will stretch your mind."

Andrew knew there would be no baseball playing unless he

cooperated. But oddly enough, Daria knew he wanted to cooperate. For the first time in Andrew's life, he wanted to "stretch his mind," as Philip called it.

Mrs. Voorhees was delighted over the change in Andrew's attitude at school and praised him in front of the other students. Daria gave her brother a big smile.

This year, the city council changed their minds about suspending last-day-of-school ceremonies. For the most part, people were learning that they had to go on living in spite of the fact that war was ravaging the country.

Though the spring had been unusually rainy, commencement day was dry, sunny, and warm. Marching bands played as all the students filled the street in a mass parade. Spectators lined the streets. Many of the convalescing soldiers stood or sat in front of the military hospital, watching the students file by. At the city square, students gave speeches and performed musical numbers.

After the picnic beneath the shade trees, the afternoon was filled with sporting events of all kinds. With Philip's help, Andrew was able to organize two full teams of players for a great game of baseball. Philip acted as an umpire and gave specific instructions about the rules. Because Andrew knew Philip personally, it made the other boys look up to him.

During the game, Andrew hit a powerful home run. As he ran to home base, Daria remembered what Roy had said—how he'd like to see Andrew run the bases in a home run. Andrew had told him he'd see it if he stuck around long enough. But Roy had chosen to leave. How Daria wished Roy had stayed home.

That evening, Uncle Jon invited the family to his home for supper. Mama insisted that their boarders come along, as well. Mr.

Martin, weary from the day's activities, declined the invitation, but Mrs. Ryan and Philip accepted.

The large Burton home was filled with guests. As Aunt Ellie put it, "There didn't seem to be anything else to celebrate, so we might as well have a party for the end of the school year."

At one point, Daria happened to be nearby when Uncle Jon was talking about a recent letter he'd received from Salmon Chase. Several persons stood about as he spoke of how Chase had gone on a journey with President Lincoln to scout out the troops and to try to discover why McClellan was hesitating in his attack.

"No one can figure out why McClellan chooses to sit on his hands doing nothing," Uncle Jon said. "Whether it's a yellow streak or not, we can't be sure. But I'm sure of one thing—it won't be long before the president takes McClellan's command from him entirely."

Out of the corner of her eye, Daria saw Mama escorting Mary Ellen hurriedly from the room. Daria didn't think Uncle Jon, surrounded by a group of men—Philip included—even noticed.

A bit later, Daria saw Philip walk out on the back porch alone. She was bored with grown-up talk, and she went to join him, thinking they might go to the stables together. She watched as Philip pulled a small notepad from his jacket and jotted down a few notes, then returned the pad to his pocket. It seemed a little strange, but then Philip was forever getting little thoughts and writing them down.

"Philip," Daria said.

"Whoa there, Daria. You ought not sneak up on an old soldier, even if he is crippled." Something in his eyes made Daria feel uneasy, but she pushed the feeling away. This was Philip, after all, their good friend.

"I didn't mean to startle you," she said. "I thought we might go look at Uncle Jon's horses."

"Let's do, Daria." Now his face looked just the same as always, and Daria was certain she had imagined whatever else she had thought she had seen there.

But why would she imagine anything in the first place? The thought made a little shiver run down her spine. After all, she trusted Philip.

Didn't she?

"You'll be pleased to know," Philip was saying, "that your uncle has offered me the loan of one of his mounts whenever I might need it as long as I'm in the city."

"Uncle Jon said that?"

"He did." Philip carefully maneuvered the steps down from the porch and onto the stone path that led to the stables. "He's a generous man, your uncle. Now I know why he's spoken of so highly."

"Uncle Jon sold a number of his horses to the government for use in the war," Daria said. "He used to keep a large herd pastured at a farm a few miles out of town. He's kept back only a few for breeding stock and for his family to ride."

Philip shook his head. "And yet he's still willing to loan one. Amazing." The corporal smoothed his mustache thoughtfully. "Well now, my young friend. When we go riding, I shan't have to put up with an old nag. What a blessing that will be. Eh?"

Daria nodded. She smiled at Philip and tried to forget that any suspicion had ever crossed her mind.

CHAPTER 13

Daria's Suspicions

Fat grasshoppers jumped out of the way in the tall grass ahead of Bordeaux as Daria and Andrew rode him up Price Hill. Behind them, Philip was mounted on Guerin, one of Uncle Jon's prime Arabians. Up away from the noise of the city, the warm June air was filled with birdcalls and the droning of insects. The three had ridden in silence for quite a ways, enjoying the peace of the summer day.

Daria and Andrew hadn't seen Philip as much recently. Their new friend was spending more time at the bookstore. While Daria was pleased that Philip's leg was healing nicely, she began to dread the day when the war would call him away. She could hardly think about it without having a lump rise up in her throat. One more thing to blame on the war. Each day, bitterness against the Confederates seemed to grow inside her.

Hearing voices up ahead, Daria knew they were drawing near to the entrenchments that the home guards had erected. No place in the city had been untouched by the war, even way up here. Price Hill gave a perfect view up and down the Ohio River, as well as across the river into Covington. Several large guns had been transported to the top of the hill and placed behind large embankments that had been dug by the men of the home guard. This was only one of a number of similar fortifications throughout the city.

Daria had often heard peevish old Mr. Martin grumble that such measures were foolish and wasteful. "We have Newport Barracks right across the river. The Rebs would have to come through whole legions of Union forces to make it to Ohio."

But the men who guarded the stations had often been fired on. Obviously, someone didn't like the idea of the city being fortified. Rumors circulated that enemy forces might land downriver and attack the city from the rear. The people of Cincinnati were terrified.

The home guard regulars had erected a shelter of poles and branches to keep the sun off and camouflage the position of the guns. Andrew called out to the guards so they would know friends were approaching. Then Daria, Andrew, and Philip dismounted and went closer to the guns to rest awhile and visit with the men.

"General Grant himself would be impressed with these guns," Philip told the two men on guard as he sat down in the shade.

"You know old Unconditional Surrender Grant?" asked one who didn't appear to be much older than Andrew and Daria.

Philip smiled and nodded. "Fought right beside him at Fort Donelson."

The boy whistled. "Sakes alive! You seen Grant?"

Philip smiled at the boy's reaction.

"That where you got that there game leg?" asked the other.

Though Philip's limp wasn't as pronounced as it once was, he still favored the leg a great deal. "That's where I got it," he answered.

The men talked of the war for a short time, and then the twins and Philip remounted and continued their leisurely Saturday afternoon ride. Each time they were together, Daria wondered if it might be the last time. The thought made her heartsick. And yet at the same time, she couldn't help but notice the way Philip's eyes looked sometimes—as though he was calculating something, something that had nothing to do with the merry expression he normally showed them.

Letters were sparse, and the mail had slowed to a snail's pace as the fighting heated up. It seemed they lived each day for the few letters that arrived. Late in June a letter from Edward told them of a battle at a place called Fair Oaks—some five miles from the Confederate capital of Richmond, Virginia—in which he had fought. He wrote:

Our camps stretch out over many acres of ground. Nearby lines of railroad cars loaded with army stores stand ready. I'm quite sure Johnny Reb hasn't nearly as much as we have in the way of food and supplies, and yet McClellan makes no move to attack Richmond. I understand there are upwards of 150,000 of us here. I may not be much of a military person, but I'm of the opinion we could take it in a day.

How can one describe battle? There were terrible rains and the Chickahominy River was swollen. Our division and two others crossed the "Grape Vine Bridge," constructed by our engineers only days before. A few feet below us rushed the flood-swollen river. There at Fair Oaks we encountered the enemy in a fierce battle. We fought in pouring rain. The musketry is terrible beyond belief, firings and explosions at every hand—like iron hail. And the cries of the wounded are the most pitiful, calling out for water or a doctor—mostly calling out to God—but there is no one to help them. We press on to continue fighting.

When it was over, the dead covered the battlefields. Long trenches are dug, and the bodies are dragged there and covered with a few inches of dirt—mud is more like it. The names of the dead, if known, are written on pieces of board.

Jenny, who was reading the letter, stopped every few sentences to press her handkerchief to her mouth to keep herself from sobbing. Then she read on.

> *As soon as the sun came out, the smell of death from the swollen bodies filled the air. The dead horses had to be burned. That smell, too, is almost unbearable. I am amazed at how our stomachs have been trained to stand the stench.*
>
> *This war is sickening, and I feel those who first started it should deserve to receive great punishment at the hand of God. Such destruction as I have seen, no man can clearly describe in its fullness.*

It was the most powerful letter they had received from the battlefront thus far. Jenny ceased reading for a moment, but none of them could speak. Mama, Daria, and Jenny were all weeping. Andrew was biting his lip and clenching his fists.

Edward's letter concluded:

> *They have erected a hospital at Fair Oaks due to the many wounded and ill. Malarious fever, scurvy, and diarrhea attack so many of our number. But there is an astounding woman named Clara Barton who works among us in battle to tend to the wounded. She is indeed an "Angel of Mercy." I have seen her holding lanterns so the surgeons can operate in the dead of night. When the men see her, somehow it sparks new bravery in their hearts.*

Edward signed off by giving his love to each person in the family. A note of a more private tone was written separately for Jenny's eyes only. As Mama did when a letter came from Papa, Jenny went off alone for a time to read it.

Daria followed her sister out into the hallway. Philip was standing there, and Daria suddenly felt certain he had been listening to Jenny read Edward's letter. Philip didn't seem to notice Daria. His eyes were on Jenny as she climbed the stairs, and Daria didn't like the expression she saw on his face. She shivered and went back in the parlor with Mama and Andrew.

That summer, much to everyone's surprise, Andrew had been reading books every evening before going to sleep. After hearing Edward's sobering letter, Andrew said he wanted to delve into a good book if only to forget the awful tone of the letter. Mama looked pleased, and Daria watched as her brother disappeared into his room with a book tucked under his arm. The title on the book's spine was *The Spy,* by Andrew's favorite author, James Fenimore Cooper. The title of the book made another nasty little chill creep over her skin. Those chilly feelings were becoming all too familiar these days.

Daria went up to her own room, but Jenny needed to be alone; and Daria slipped out again, leaving her sister to read through Edward's letter for the tenth time. Jenny needed her privacy, Daria knew. Besides, something was bothering Daria, something she needed to discuss with her twin. With her wrapper over her nightgown and her long hair, free of braids, hanging about her shoulders, she tiptoed downstairs and knocked softly on Andrew's door.

"I'm sorry, ma'am," Andrew joked, "but the doctor's out just now. Won't you come back at a more opportune time?"

But Daria didn't laugh as she usually did. "Might I talk with you a moment, Andrew?"

Andrew opened the door wider. "I wasn't exactly prepared for company. The tea's not quite steeped, but do come in."

Daria managed a weak smile, and watched as Andrew went into Papa's office and brought out his desk chair. He motioned Daria to it; then he plopped down on his bed.

"Care for an apple?" He pointed to the bowl.

Daria shook her head. She was quiet for a moment, searching for the words to say what was on her mind. She knew Andrew wasn't going to like what she had to say.

She studied her hands in her lap for a time. Finally, she said, "Andrew, do you believe in intuition?"

Andrew thought a moment. "Like a sense that you know something?"

She nodded.

"Sometimes I feel like I know what you're thinking before you say it," Andrew said. "Is that what you mean?"

"More than that. Like you feel something, but there's no real facts or proof to back it up."

"This isn't about Papa, is it? You don't have a feeling about Papa, do you?" Daria could read the fear in Andrew's face. She knew he sometimes had nightmares about Papa being wounded. . .or worse.

"No, no," she hurried to say. "Not about Papa. Something else."

"Well, what then?"

Daria hesitated again, then said in a rush, "Andrew, you think a lot of Philip Harnden, don't you? I mean, he's become a good friend to you."

"A very good friend—to all of us. You, too. You don't think he's in danger, do you?"

She studied her hands again, hating to say anything more. Andrew was right, of course. She had come to consider Philip Harnden a good friend. That's what made her suspicions so terribly painful. "I don't think he's in danger," she said slowly. "Something deep inside tells me he may be causing danger."

Andrew felt his throat tighten. "I'm sure he causes a lot of danger for those wicked Rebs out on that battlefield."

"That's not what I mean. I've had a feeling about him lately,

Andrew. Sometimes he gets this look on his face. And tonight, earlier, I saw him looking at Jenny—"

"Daria Ann Fisk," Andrew interrupted, "you stop that talk right now. You've got no call to talk about Philip like that. He's not even here to defend himself. He'd never be anything but a gentleman. Besides, I thought you really liked him. You've spent a lot of time together."

"I do really like him," Daria said miserably. "At least most of the time. But have you noticed the way he's so interested in all the goings-on of the city? Every detail—from the news that Uncle Jon received from Salmon Chase, to the troop movements from Christian. And he has a little notebook that he keeps things jotted down in. I've seen him."

Andrew looked as though he were struggling to curb an explosion of anger at his sister. "Of course he's interested. Soon he'll be return-ing to his men, and he needs to know what's going on there. Daria, you've been eating too many green apples or something. It's touched you in the head."

Daria stood to go. "I'm sorry I came to you," she said stiffly. "In the old days, we could tell each other anything. And you always trusted me more than anybody. What's changed?"

Andrew didn't meet her eyes. "I guess we're just growing up," he muttered.

Daria bit her lips to keep back her own hurt and anger. After a moment, she said as calmly as she could, "I waited for my feeling, my intuition, to go away. I kept hoping it would. I've prayed and prayed that I'm wrong. But the feeling is still here." She placed her hand over her stomach. "Deep in here. As much as I want to, I can't shake it."

"Well, your feeling is wrong. Dead wrong. I can tell you that for certain. I don't even want to talk about this anymore. You'd better go on back to bed."

"At least pray about it. Will you do that?" She felt funny saying the words. Just a few months ago, it would have been Andrew telling her to pray.

"Of course, Daria. I'll pray."

For a moment, Daria felt relieved. Maybe she could leave this with God, the way Mama was always saying they should do about anything that worried them. Then she happened to glance down at her brother's hand. Andrew had crossed his fingers. Her heart sank. She knew her brother had no intention of praying.

Daria couldn't sleep that night. She tossed and turned all night long, fighting and fighting against her suspicions. She had never ever seen her twin so angry at her. Yet Daria knew that she had to tell someone. She hated how she felt. Andrew was right; Philip had been a good friend, and she had enjoyed spending time with him. He was a touch of Papa. But she just couldn't make the odd feeling inside her go away. Something about Philip just wasn't right.

The next morning at breakfast, she noticed that Andrew couldn't even bring himself to look at her. His eyes were angry and his mouth was set in a straight line. Daria hated how much she had hurt him.

Devastating news arrived in Cincinnati just before the big July Fourth celebration. General Lee had routed the Union forces, driving them back from Richmond, Virginia. Everyone who was crowded about the newspaper office was disgusted and discouraged.

Daria wondered how much more the country could take. The horrific battle had begun on June 25 and ended on July 1—the longest running battle of the war so far. And for what? Victory seemed further and further away. Who would have thought those few little states in the

South would fight with such pluck and audacity?

No letters came from Edward. For several days, Jenny appeared to be on the brink of tears nearly every waking moment. It broke Daria's heart to see her so distraught.

Meanwhile, both by telegraph and by word of mouth, rumors spread of raids in Kentucky led by Colonel John Hunt Morgan. Brazenly, he struck at federal supply points and destroyed railroad tracks and bridges. He took control of telegraph offices, breaking off important communications. These hit-and-run raids had Cincinnati panicked.

Then one day, Colonel Morgan and his men actually moved into Kentucky. By July 9, he'd taken Tompkinsville and Glasgow. There wasn't much to stop him from pressing through Kentucky, crossing the Ohio River, and taking over Cincinnati.

CHAPTER 14

The War Approaches

A few days later, after time had helped heal some of the wounds between the twins, Daria and Andrew went into town. Daria felt swallowed up in the press of the crowd milling about the Court Street marketplace. On a makeshift platform stood Judge Hugh Jewett, giving a speech to the mass of alarmed citizens. He appealed for recruits to help defend Kentucky. Large numbers of men were lining up.

Ohio's Governor Dennison also addressed the group. He explained that troops from Fort Chase had already been sent to Lexington, Kentucky, and that most of the Cincinnati police force was to be sent out, as well.

Daria felt surrounded by fear and panic. No one had ever thought the war would come this far north. They'd been lulled into a false sense of security as the war raged miles away. The citizens were confused and frustrated by the conflicting reports of where Colonel Morgan and his men were located. Some said he was pretending to prepare for an attack on Lexington so he could come north another way undetected. Others said he was making a beeline for Cincinnati with thousands of men.

Daria and Andrew remained in town for a couple of hours, watching all the activities unfolding. As the afternoon grew late, though, they knew they needed to get back to Walnut Hills to report the situation to Mama. Most of the crowds were beginning to thin out anyway.

"Let's ask Philip what he thinks," Andrew suggested. He met

Daria's eyes as though he were daring her to argue.

What could she say? She knew Andrew refused to share her suspicions. With a shrug, she followed Andrew out of the marketplace and to the bookstore where Philip worked.

The cool, dim interior of the bookstore gave instant relief from the July heat. Daria looked around for Philip, but he didn't seem to be there. She remembered he'd said that morning he'd be very busy at the store because a new shipment of books was arriving.

A stooped, gray-haired man with dimming eyesight approached Daria and Andrew. Adjusting his eyeglasses and peering up at Daria, he said, "Might I be of assistance? Are you looking for any book in particular?"

"We're looking for Philip Harnden."

"Oh." The man studied Daria and Andrew even more closely. "Just a moment, please." And he went to the back room.

In a moment, another man came out of the back room. He had the look of a gambler, with a starched linen shirt and a purple satin vest decorated with a gold watch chain. His hair was carefully parted and combed back. "You're looking for Philip?" he asked.

"Yes. We needed to speak with him for a moment."

"I'm sorry, but he just stepped out."

"Will he be gone long? We could wait," Andrew said.

"It might be an hour or so," the man replied, pulling out the gold watch from his satin vest.

"I guess you're having to put up the shipment of books all by yourselves then," Daria said.

"Shipment of books? Oh, yes, the shipment. Yes, we're taking care of all that."

Suddenly, Andrew looked as though a terrible thought had occurred to him. "He didn't go to rejoin his men, did he? Or to go to Lexington with the volunteers?"

The man smiled. "Oh, my, no. Not with his bad leg."

But Daria knew Philip was walking better on his leg each day. She nudged Andrew. "I guess we'd better go home. Will you tell him we came by?"

"Your names, please?"

"I'm Daria Fisk, and this is my brother, Andrew."

"Ah, yes. The young Fisks. He's spoken of you. We'll tell him you stopped by."

Daria and Andrew left the bookstore. "That's funny," Andrew said. "If Philip was out on an errand, why didn't those men invite us to wait?"

And why, Daria wondered silently, *did the man hesitate when I mentioned the shipment of books?* And why was a man who worked in a bookstore dressed in a purple satin vest? It certainly seemed strange.

At home, Daria and Andrew reported all the news to Mama and Jenny, who had just returned from the hospital, where they'd been working throughout the day. They'd heard bits and pieces of the threat of attack. It was grim news indeed. None of them could even imagine having their city taken over by Rebel forces.

That evening, Daria took Andrew aside. "Have you even thought about what I said the other night?"

Andrew looked unhappy. "Some."

"Don't you think that those men at the bookstore acted a little strange? How about if we create a little test for Philip?"

"What kind of test?"

"A test to see whether or not Philip's been telling the truth all along."

Andrew shook his head. "That's devious. I don't want to be any part of it."

"Then don't be. Just stand by and listen. Will you do that much?"

Andrew didn't answer. But he didn't say no.

When Philip came home that evening, he went right to Daria and Andrew and apologized for being away when they had stopped by. "Judge Jewett asked that I brief a few of the recruits before they left for Kentucky. I felt it was the least I could do in light of the circumstances. Some of those men are green as a gourd."

Andrew smiled and looked at Daria, as though to say, *See? I knew Philip would have a good reason for being out.*

"The men in the store didn't seem to know where you went," Daria said.

Philip gave a little laugh. "I heard the alarm bells sounding, and then a man came in saying there might be martial law. Knowing they would need help, I grabbed my hat and ran. Didn't have time to say anything to anyone."

Andrew looked relieved, but Daria didn't find Philip's explanation quite so convincing.

At supper, everyone discussed what was going on in Kentucky, but Philip didn't seem to know any more than the rest of them. He did comment that the Rebels would never be able to make it past the forces either in Lexington or Covington. "The entrenchments are well laid out," he said confidently.

That night as usual, Philip joined Andrew and Daria in the stable to groom Bordeaux. Together, they mucked out the stall and put out clean straw.

Mama was insisting that Daria wear a hooped petticoat under her dresses these days, and Daria found it difficult to work in the stable when her every step was hampered by the bouncy hoop. Finally, Daria gave up. She pulled out a tack box, adjusted her hoop, and sat down. This was as good a time as any to try her test on Philip.

She swallowed back her nervousness and said, "Andrew says that when he misses Papa, being with Bordeaux seems to help."

"I see," Philip said. Andrew kept on brushing. Daria knew he didn't want to even look at her.

"I've been missing Papa something awful tonight," Daria went on. "It's been so long since we had a letter." She paused a moment as though for emphasis. "It seems strange that you've seen Papa since we have, Philip."

"I was blessed to be given the opportunity."

Andrew looked over Bordeaux's back and gave Daria a warning glare, but she avoided his eyes. "I love to remember the nice things about Papa, like the way he always removed his eyeglasses when he was talking to us. Or," she paused again, "the way he tapped his pipe out thoughtfully."

Andrew peeked over at her again, trying to give her his angriest scowl. She wouldn't look at him.

"I wonder, Andrew, if Papa was able to hang on to the fine pipe we gave him. Tell me, Philip, did Papa have his nice meerschaum pipe when you saw him in camp?"

"He surely did, Miss Daria. That pipe was like it was a part of him."

Daria felt a grim satisfaction. Papa abhorred any and all uses of tobacco. He'd never touched a pipe in his life. She heard Andrew make an odd little choking noise, but she covered it with a cough.

"Do you think he made it through the battle at Donelson with his pipe?" she went on.

"Can't say for sure," Philip answered nonchalantly. "Most soldiers lost much of their gear during a battle. But your papa would have been in the medical tents behind the lines, so I'm willing to guess he's still puffing on that special pipe."

Daria suddenly felt as though she were going to be sick. She jumped up from the tack box. "Goodness, I just remembered. Mama asked me to fill the lamps, and I totally forgot. I don't want to think about how much trouble I'll be in if I don't get it done quickly. Good night, Philip." Daria looked straight at Andrew. "Good night, Andrew."

Daria waited until midnight, when she was certain everyone in the house would be asleep, and then she tiptoed down the stairs to Andrew's bedroom. He let her in as though he'd been waiting for her, but then he flopped back down on his bed and didn't even offer her a chair. "Think you're pretty smart, don't you?" His voice sounded almost as though he had been crying. "But you're not, you know. There are so many soldiers and so many officers! Philip could be mixed up. He might have Papa confused with another surgeon."

Daria looked at her brother sadly. "One who just happens to smoke a meerschaum pipe?"

Andrew seemed confused for a moment, but then he said stubbornly, "He was just trying to be kind, Daria. He didn't want you to be disappointed." He looked at his twin defiantly. "You don't have to be so smug about it!"

Daria stepped backward as though her brother had slapped her. "Andrew, I didn't want to find out Philip Harnden is an imposter. Do you think I did?"

"I don't know what to think. But I know there are hundreds and hundreds of men in a camp. He would never remember about one little pipe with all the war and everything. He was just going along with you to be nice."

Daria let out a big sigh. "Is that what you believe? Truly?"

"Truly," he answered.

"Very well, then. I've never seen you be so taken with a person. Nothing I could say would ever make any difference." She turned to go.

With her hand on the doorknob, she added, "I thought you trusted me more than that. I am your sister—your twin. But I guess that doesn't matter anymore."

CHAPTER 15
Martial Law

Colonel Morgan's threats of an attack were like a dress rehearsal. The real thing came in late August.

On Saturday night, August 30, Daria and Andrew hurried into town to get the latest news. General Kirby Smith's forces had driven northward all the way to Richmond—not the capital of Virginia, but a village just south of Lexington, Kentucky. What few Union troops he had met along the way were raw recruits barely able to reload their muskets. They had quickly fled.

Panic hit Cincinnati. There was talk that Frankfort and Lexington might have to be abandoned to the enemy.

Daria and Andrew had to bring home the news that this threat was genuine. The next morning, Andrew rode Bordeaux back into town to see how he could help. Word was that Colonel Morgan had joined General Smith. Kentuckians who still sided with the South were cheering them on and aiding the Rebel forces with food and supplies all along the way. Cincinnati's mayor announced a citywide council meeting that evening to map out plans for defending the city against attack. At church that morning, the mood was grim.

That evening, Andrew hitched up the buggy and took Mr. Martin and Philip to the council meeting. When they came home, they reported that General Lewis Wallace would oversee Cincinnati's defense. General Wallace had fought at Shiloh and made a good showing for himself. He had been in charge of troops at Lexington.

After the council meeting, the general was to meet privately with the mayors of Newport, Covington, and Cincinnati to devise a plan.

That night no one could sleep. Finally, everyone gathered in the parlor to discuss the news. Mirza stopped by, as well, and fixed them lemonade, and Mama invited her to join them.

Andrew told Mama, "Whatever they need to get done, I'm ready to help."

Mama just nodded.

Daria looked around the room and realized that someone was missing. "Where's Philip?" she asked.

"Most likely he's with the officers, deploying new recruits," Andrew said confidently. He looked right at Daria as he said it.

Mr. Martin kept shaking his head and saying, "I never thought they'd come this far north."

Mama got out the Bible and read the Ninety-first Psalm. " 'I will say of the LORD, he is my refuge and my fortress: my God; in him will I trust,' " she quoted. Everyone seemed comforted by these words.

When the mantel gong clock struck two, Mama ordered everyone to bed. "Let's see if we can get a little sleep," she told them. "There'll be plenty for all of us to do in the days ahead."

The next morning, Andrew collected as many papers as he could and brought them back to the house. They all contained General Wallace's proclamation, which placed Cincinnati under martial law, with the federal military taking responsibility for the city's safety.

"How will that affect us?" Daria asked.

"It says here," Jenny explained as she skimmed the paper, "that all businesses will close and remain closed until further notice; all citizens must be assembled by 10:00 a.m. to receive orders for work; and all ferry boats will stop running until further notice."

The governor of Ohio was staying in Cincinnati. He telegraphed his adjutant general to send messages to all the rural areas of the state, asking every available man who owned a gun to come to Cincinnati and help defend the city. As a result, alarm bells rang throughout the countryside of Ohio.

By nightfall, volunteers began arriving by trainloads. Hundreds of backwoodsmen in homespun shirts and trousers, carrying their powder horns, buckskin pouches, and long muskets, converged on the city.

Mama, Daria, and Jenny helped cook meals for the "Squirrel Hunters," as the folks in Cincinnati called these volunteers. The men were housed in halls, warehouses, and anywhere else where there was room. They were greeted with cheers and treated like royalty. For a time, all was forgotten but the work of fortifying the city. Everyone knew that at any moment the enemy might attack.

Daria knew that Andrew didn't sleep or even stop by the house for the first twenty-four hours while he was helping to build a pontoon bridge. Once it was finished, he was set to work building breastworks and rifle pits on the other side of the river. Finally, late in the afternoon of the second day of the siege, Andrew came home. He said an older worker had insisted he go get some rest. Knowing he couldn't hold out much longer, Andrew had reluctantly done as he was told.

Just after Andrew came through the door, Philip came in, as well. "Andrew, I've been looking for you."

"I've been helping with the work. Where've you been?"

"Why, with the recruits, of course. Can we talk?"

Andrew's eyes were bleary with weariness. "What is it, Philip?"

"The time's come, Andrew." Philip turned toward Daria and shrugged. "I must go. My regiment needs me."

Daria thought her brother looked as though he'd been hit—hit hard. She felt relieved that Philip would no longer be under their roof where she felt obliged to always keep an eye on him—but her heart hurt for her brother. She knew how much he had come to love this man.

"The whole of Kentucky has exploded," Philip said. "I'm some better now. I may not be able to march, but I'll report back to my commanding officer to see what I can do to help."

Andrew nodded, but Daria saw that his eyes were wet.

"I'm all packed and ready to go, but I need to ask you something, Andrew, Daria." He looked from one twin to the other. "Something I could never ask anyone other than close friends like you."

"What is it?" Andrew asked in a hoarse whisper.

"I need Bordeaux."

"Bordeaux?" Andrew's voice croaked.

"Andrew, I need a horse. Time is of the essence. You know what the railroads are like right now. And the ferries are closed down." He gave a little shrug and a smile. "I'd walk if I could."

"He's not really mine to give. He's Papa's horse. Daria and I are responsible for him."

Daria's mind was reeling. How could Andrew even consider giving up Bordeaux? What would Mama say? And Papa?

"I need to ask Mama. I must ask her."

At least, Daria thought, her brother still had enough sense left to insist on talking to Mama. She held her own tongue, afraid that all her anger and suspicion would come spilling out were she to speak.

"Where is your mother?"

"At the Fifth Street Market House, where they're feeding the soldiers," Daria said. "They've been there all day. I could ride back into town to ask her." That would keep Bordeaux safely away from Philip's clutches.

As she spoke, they heard the clatter of a carriage out front. Daria went to the window, relieved to see Uncle Jon's carriage. Better yet, she could see that Mama and Jenny were inside.

Philip smiled again, his eyes crinkling. "Perfect timing," he said. "Just perfect."

"Let me go ask," Andrew said, his voice so faint Daria could barely hear it.

"I'll come with you," Philip offered.

Daria shook her head. "We'd better ask her alone. She's going to be upset."

"Whatever you say," Philip said.

As they walked toward their mother, Daria's mind was racing. How could she explain her suspicions to Mama? She glanced sideways at her brother. Surely now he would believe her.

Andrew's face was very pale. "Everybody's had to make sacrifices," he said. "It will hurt. But we can do it. We'll get by." He sounded as though he were trying to convince himself.

"How can you still believe him?" Daria asked, but Andrew gave her such a fierce look that she shut her mouth and was silent. She trailed behind as Andrew called Mama and Jenny into the parlor, where he explained Philip's request.

Immediately, Mama said, "Well, of course we'll give him the horse. I know you love Bordeaux. We all do. And Papa does, as well. But there will be other horses. If this will help the corporal get back to where he needs to be, then the horse is his."

Solemnly, Andrew nodded.

Daria felt sick inside. She grabbed the back of her brother's shirt and kept him from leaving the room. "Don't do this, Andrew," she whispered urgently. "Please, please don't do this. Don't let that man leave on our horse. Tell Mama what I suspect."

Andrew turned and gave Daria a hard shove, knocking her off balance. "Get away from me! Can't you see how much harder you're making this?" He stomped out the door, tears running down his cheeks.

Daria stood stunned. How could this happen? Should she try to tell Mama?

But she knew there wasn't time. She forced herself to run after Andrew, but she reached the stable just in time to hear Andrew say simply, "He's yours."

Philip stretched out his hand. "Thank you, Andrew. You're a true friend."

In a few minutes, Philip had his bags secured behind the saddle and was mounted. "This old war will be over soon, Andrew. And when it is, we'll have a baseball game to end all baseball games." He gave Daria a jaunty wave.

Daria felt as though she were trapped in a nightmare. She watched while Mama and Jenny stood on the front porch and waved good-bye. As Bordeaux trotted away from them, she realized the saddle that Papa had given them was on the horse. She started to say something, but Andrew seemed to read her mind, the way he always did. "What does it matter?" he asked dully. "If there will be other horses, then there will be other saddles."

He ran back into the stable. Daria followed him more slowly. She came inside in time to see him fling himself into the hay and sob like a baby. She had meant to yell at her twin, but when she saw Andrew crying, her heart broke for him.

"Andrew," she said softly, "it'll be all right. God will watch over Bordeaux and Philip." Somehow, in spite of everything, for the first time she really believed this. She turned to go back into the house. Daria knew there was really nothing she could say to make Andrew feel better right now.

CHAPTER 16

The Spy Ring

"Andrew? Are you still in there? Andrew?" Daria called.

"Go away," he muttered sleepily. Daria knew her twin didn't want to see her. He probably didn't want to see anyone. But she had to talk to him.

"I have something to show you."

"I don't want to see."

She pushed the door open anyway and came in with a lantern in one hand and a folded piece of paper in the other.

Slowly he sat up. "What time is it?"

"Almost nine. You've been asleep for a long time." She sat down on the floor of the stable. "Andrew," she said gently, "look at this. I found it in Philip's room. Behind his bureau."

Andrew scowled. "You searched his room?"

"Just look at it."

The paper was on bookstore business stationery. On it were drawings of troop movements, troop locations, and troop sizes. Andrew shook his head. "Daria, you silly goose. Everybody is interested in troop movements these days. I don't know what you're trying to prove."

Daria yanked the paper from his hands. "Andrew Fisk, you're determined not to believe a thing I say. Well, I'm going into town and have a look around that so-called bookstore."

"Mama would never let you do such a thing."

"Mama's exhausted, and she's sound asleep. She'll never know I'm gone."

Andrew sighed. Then he brushed hay off himself and stood up. "Wait a minute and I'll go with you. There are troops swarming all over town. If you got in any trouble, I'd never hear the end of it."

Grabbing his hat, Andrew joined Daria and they hurried off to town. "I'm dead tired," he complained under his breath, "and now you're making me walk all the way back into town just because of your foolish suspicions. . . ." He heaved another huge sigh, as though all the troubles of the world had settled on his shoulders. "This is not how I wanted to spend my evening," he grumbled, but he sounded more like his old self now. Daria knew he would stay with her, if only to prove her wrong.

In town, it was as busy as if it were midday. Soldiers were everywhere. Daria and Andrew figured if anyone stopped them, they would just say that they were on their way to their aunt and uncle's house. But no one did. They made their way to Third Street, then turned and went down the alley behind the bookstore.

Although she was sure that there was something wrong, Daria felt silly. She didn't even know what she was looking for. But after she'd gone only a few feet, she knew exactly what she was looking for. She and Andrew stopped short.

There was Bordeaux tied in the alley. But his blaze was gone. It had been blacked over.

Quietly, Daria and Andrew stepped up to their beloved horse. Bordeaux nickered softly. Daria patted his nose. "Philip left hours ago," she whispered. "Why didn't he take you with him like he said?"

Ducking down, Daria and Andrew crawled up to a small window that was open. There in the back room of the bookstore several men had gathered. Daria recognized two of them as the old man and the dandy they'd seen in the bookstore the day they were looking for Philip. Her heart pounded. What was going on?

Just then, in through a side door came a sandy-haired, clean-shaven man dressed in a smart-looking federal uniform complete with saber and sheath and the insignia of a lieutenant.

Andrew reached out and grabbed Daria's arm as though to steady himself. The lieutenant was Philip Harnden—and he walked with no limp!

Turning to the older man, Philip said, "Frank, your disguises are getting better and better. This uniform fits like a glove."

The older man he called Frank was riffling through papers on a desk. "Here's your pass to get you across the river, Michael, and here are your military papers, all in order."

"At first," said the dandy, "I thought all this uproar would put us in a pinch, but now it seems to be working in our favor. The extra soldiers in town will make it even easier for you to slip away."

"Especially with the pontoon bridge," added Philip. "What a stroke of luck. They made a highway especially for my departure."

One of the other men with his back to the window said, "Give General Smith our regards, Michael. Tell him we'll continue to gather information here and funnel it to him as best we can."

"It won't be quite as good without Michael here," put in another.

"Your grays are in the bag on the horse," said Frank. "Your contact in Lexington will tell you when and where it'll be safe to change."

Daria thought Andrew looked like he was going to be sick. Daria had been right all along, but now that she knew for certain that Philip Harnden—or Michael—was a dirty spy, she felt like she might throw up, too. But she knew they had to do something—and do it quickly. Maybe they could fetch a policeman or a federal officer before Philip could get away.

But as they turned to go, Daria was grabbed from behind. A big smelly hand clamped over her mouth, and her arms were jerked painfully behind her back. Beside her, she could tell that Andrew had

133

met with the same fate. As Daria struggled and kicked, she was dragged over to a door and pushed inside.

Inside, all eyes turned toward the children. The big man who was holding Daria said, "Looka here what we found outside the window."

Philip's face went white. "Daria! Andrew!" he said softly.

Daria tried to look sideways at her brother, but all she could see were his legs wiggling and struggling. He must have forced his face up out of his captor's grasp, for Daria heard him choke out, "Dirty, filthy Rebel spy! I trusted you, you traitor! Our whole family trusted you! I hate you!" A hand must have clamped down again on his mouth, and Daria's twin was forced to fall silent.

"What'll we do with them?" asked the big man.

Philip's eyes were sad. "You shouldn't have followed me," he said to the twins. "I'd hoped it wouldn't come to this." To the other men he said, "Tie them up, gag them, and put them in the storage closet. Don't let them out until I'm long gone and you've gotten rid of all the evidence. Then move our headquarters. They'll cause no trouble."

While the men tied and gagged Andrew and Daria, the others prepared to leave.

"You all know your assignments," Frank told them. "There's no reason why this shouldn't go as smooth as silk. We'll meet back here in an hour."

With the gag tearing at her mouth and the ropes cutting into her wrists, Daria was thrown into a dark closet. In a second, Andrew fell on top of her.

"Be careful with them," she heard Philip say.

The door closed, and it was pitch dark. There were footsteps and the sounds of doors closing, then Daria heard Frank's voice saying, "We'll have to get rid of the young'uns."

The dandy answered, "I know. But not until Michael's long gone. He doesn't need to know."

Then it was quiet. Daria couldn't stop the tears running down her cheeks. She couldn't even brush them away.

Beside her, she could hear Andrew snuffling, as though he were trying not to cry, too. Daria suddenly felt angry. These Rebel spies couldn't be allowed to succeed. She had to do something. She struggled with the rope around her wrists. To her surprise, she found it wasn't quite as tight as it had seemed at first. She knew her hands were more slender than her twin's. When they lost a marble or a piece of paper behind some piece of furniture, Daria was always the one who could squeeze her hand small enough to fit. Maybe. . .just maybe. . . She wriggled and twisted her fingers, making her hands squeeze as tiny as she could possibly make them. The rough rope bit at her skin, and she could feel warm blood trickling down her wrists, but she refused to give up. With a little gasp of pain and one last terrible effort, she tugged one hand free.

For a moment, she could only sit frozen, hardly able to believe she had really done it. Then she yanked off her gag and reached for Andrew's. She couldn't see him in the dark, but she could feel his warm breath on her face as she fumbled with the rest of their bonds.

"They're all spies," Andrew choked as soon as he could speak. "You were right." Daria thought he still sounded as though he might cry. "I wanted so much to help in the war—but all I did was feed information to the enemy. When I think of all the strategic places we took Philip, all the influential people we introduced him to. . . He was just using us the whole time!" Andrew choked back a sob. "The worst part is that I trusted him more than I did my own sister." His hand reached out for Daria's. "Can you forgive me?"

Daria squeezed her brother's fingers. "Of course. But we need to stop him."

"Let's go!" Andrew no longer sounded as though he was going to cry.

The children pushed open the closet door, then climbed through the window and ran down the alley. When they reached the street, they flagged down a sentry officer on horseback.

"What are you kids doing out at this time of night? Don't you know there's a war on? Hey, aren't you Dr. Fisk's children?"

"We are. Take us to the landing," Daria told him. "There's a Rebel spy who has our horse. He's dressed as a lieutenant, and he's carrying forged papers."

The officer reached down and helped Andrew mount behind him, then gave Daria a hand up to sit in front of him. Quickly, he guided the horse through the darkened streets to the landing. Daria could only hope they weren't too late.

Even at that late hour, the landing was crowded with soldiers and civilians who were working to defend the city.

"Do you see him?" asked the officer.

Daria wondered if they'd ever find Philip among so many people. Perhaps he had already gotten across the river to the safety of Kentucky.

Suddenly, Daria spied Philip, sitting tall and proud on Bordeaux. He was talking with a guard near the bridge. The guard was looking over the papers.

"That's him," Daria told the officer. "The lieutenant by the bridge!"

"Detain that man!" the officer shouted to the guard.

A startled Philip Harnden looked in their direction, then yanked Bordeaux's reins to make a break for it down the landing and through the crowd. The guard shouted for other guards to join the chase.

Thinking fast, Daria shouted, "Bordeaux! Come, boy!" Then Andrew gave his whistle, the special whistle that Bordeaux always answered. The horse tossed his head and stopped short halfway down the landing. A mounted guard caught up and pulled a gun on Philip Harnden, ordering him to dismount. The Rebel spy was quickly relieved of his weapons.

Daria and Andrew scrambled down from the horse, thanking the officer for his help. Looking down at them, the young officer said, "I believe you're the ones who should be thanked."

At gunpoint, Philip was brought back to where the young Fisks were standing.

"He's part of a ring of spies," Andrew told them. "The headquarters is at the bookstore on Third Street. They create disguises and falsify papers there. He's been in the city on a spy mission for several months calling himself Philip Harnden. But they called him Michael."

The officer said to the soldiers nearby, "Get over to that bookstore and stand guard outside until we can investigate."

The guard looked at Philip Harnden and shook his head. "Never would have thought it." Then he motioned with his gun for Philip to move. "Let's go, Reb."

"Could I have just a minute?" Philip asked.

"Make it snappy," said the guard. "We want to lock the likes of you away in a federal prison as soon as possible."

Looking at Andrew and Daria with sad eyes, Philip said softly, "I didn't count on you being such fine people, Daria and Andrew. Or that we'd become such close friends. You made my difficult assignment even more difficult."

In a voice that cracked, Andrew asked, "How am I supposed to believe that? You've lied to me about everything. You probably never even played baseball."

Daria moved closer to Andrew's side until her shoulder was next to his.

"I've played baseball. But not in Chicago. You'll be a great player one day, Andrew." He paused then, and Daria could see the tears forming in the man's eyes. "I've wished many times that I truly had met Dr. Kevin Fisk. He must be one fine man to have children such as you. I know he must be extremely proud."

Daria could not stop her own hot tears. How she wanted to hate this man, but she could not. She grabbed her brother's hand and held on tight. At least they still had each other. And God had watched out for Bordeaux, just as she had believed He would.

"Someday you'll understand why I did what I did," Philip continued. "I obeyed orders just as your father obeys orders. Just as Edward and Christian obey orders. It's the way of war."

He took a step closer to Daria and Andrew. "When this wretched war is over, I'd like to come back and see you, Daria. To see all your family—your wonderful family."

For a moment longer Daria held on to the bitterness that had built inside her for so long. This man represented everything she hated about the war. But then she knew that Papa was right. They had to rise above the war somehow. They could not let it take root in their hearts. She swallowed hard and nodded.

"And maybe play a game of baseball." Philip reached out to shake Andrew's hand.

Daria found she was glad when Andrew reached out his hand, as well. He sounded as though he were choking out the words as he said, "I think I'd like that—Michael."

"Come on," the guard growled. "Enough of all that."

Watching Philip being led away, Daria remembered Papa's prayer that none of his family would allow hate to rule their hearts. God had answered that prayer.

Andrew looked at his sister and smiled. "Thanks, Daria."

She wrapped her arms around his chest and squeezed him tight. She knew now that no matter how old they grew or where life took them, they would never lose each other.

CHAPTER 17

Roy Returns

The Rebel forces in Kentucky never arrived at Cincinnati. A few days later, martial law ended, businesses opened again, and life returned to normal. At least as normal as life ever got during the war.

General Wallace heaped praise upon the citizens. At the family breakfast table, Daria read the letter published in the *Gazette*, which said:

> *When I assumed command, there was nothing to defend you with, except a few half-finished works and some dismounted guns; yet I was confident. . . . You were appealed to. The answer will never be forgotten.*
>
> *Paris may have seen something like it with her revolutionary days, but the cities of America never did. Be proud that you have given them an example so splendid. . . . You have won much honor.*
>
> *Lewis Wallace,*
> *Major General Commanding*

Later, Daria read that Kirby Smith had never been ordered to attack Cincinnati. By September 12, all General Smith's Rebel troops were in a quick retreat. The next day, the governor sent all the Squirrel Hunters home, the thanks of the people of Cincinnati ringing in their ears.

A few weeks later, Daria hurried up the steps of the military hospital ahead of Mama and Andrew. She was scared, nervous, and excited all at the same time. They'd just received word by messenger that Roy had been wounded—taking a musket ball in the shoulder—and that he'd arrived home on the early morning train.

As they stepped into the dim hospital lobby, Daria saw a couple coming toward them, and she recognized Mr. and Mrs. Gartner. Mr. Gartner's arm was around his wife as she wept and leaned heavily on him.

Andrew ran up to them. "Is Roy here? Is he all right?"

Mrs. Gartner nodded and tried to speak, but words wouldn't come.

"He's in the ward on the third floor," Mr. Gartner said. "And he's fine. That's why Emily here is weeping. Our boy is safe and he's home."

Mrs. Gartner, dabbing at her tears with a handkerchief, said, "He's a hero. Roy is a hero." She sniffed again. "He was supposed to stay at the rear, but he threw down his drum and ran to help a friend. When he saw the friend was dead, he picked up his musket and shot a Rebel sniper." She couldn't continue, so Mr. Gartner finished.

"Killing the sniper saved the life of a Union officer, and they gave Roy a field promotion. He's a sergeant now!"

That was all Daria could bear to hear. Forgetting her manners, she ran toward the stairs and flew up to the third floor. In no time, she was by Roy's side. Their old friend was much thinner and looked years older. Though pale and weary, he managed a smile.

"Welcome home, Sergeant Gartner," Andrew said as he came up beside Daria. He reached out to shake Roy's hand.

"Good to be home. I musta been touched in the head to want to go to war, Andrew. It ain't nothin' like I thought it'd be. No glory. It's just death and dying, that's all." His face puckered. "Killing a man is a terrible thing."

Mama joined them then, and she also welcomed Roy home. He winced as he smiled at them and thanked them for coming. Daria could tell he was in pain.

"I read the story of how you two broke up a real Rebel spy ring right here in the city," Roy said. "The paper said Andrew even got a commendation and a medal. Can I see it?"

Daria and Andrew smiled. This boy who'd survived battle after battle wanted to see Andrew's little medal? Andrew jabbed a thumb toward Daria. "I gave it to my sister. If it hadn't been for her, the spies would have gotten away, and we might not be having this conversation. She was the one who earned the medal."

"In my way of thinking, you're all heroes," Mama put in. "Come now," she said to the twins. "Let's allow Roy to rest. We can come back again tomorrow."

"Yes," Andrew agreed. "I want him to get well so we can get a baseball team formed." To Roy he said, "And I have a genuine rule book now."

"A baseball game sounds mighty inviting just now," Roy said wearily. "Mighty inviting."

Three days after Daria and Andrew turned thirteen, President Abraham Lincoln issued a decree that freed all the slaves. As Daria read the words of the Emancipation Proclamation from the newspaper the next morning, she felt hope for the first time in months. Surely if the slaves were free, there would be nothing more to fight about. No more blood needed to be shed.

"Will this end it, Mama?" she asked, looking across the table at her mother. "Will this finally end the war?"

"I don't know, Daria. No one knows." Mama smiled sadly. "But whatever the future holds, we must trust God to be with us and with those we love."

Daria looked at the chair where Papa used to sit. She thought of Edward and Christian and what they might be facing that very morning. Mama was right. The war might end tomorrow. It might last for years. But for today, Daria knew what to do. She bowed her head and silently prayed for her family and for the families of everyone fighting in the war. And she said a special prayer for her country.

If you enjoyed

Daria
Solves a Mystery

be sure to read other

SISTERS IN TIME

books from BARBOUR PUBLISHING

- Perfect for Girls Ages Eight to Twelve

- History and Faith in Intriguing Stories

- Lead Character Overcomes Personal Challenge

- Covers Seventeenth to Twentieth Centuries

- Collectible Series of Titles

6" x 8 ¼" / Paperback / 144 pages / $3.97

AVAILABLE WHEREVER CHRISTIAN BOOKS ARE SOLD.